Nineveh
IRAN
Zagros Mountains
Tigris
P O T A M I A
Baghdad
Sippar
Babylon
Nippur
Isin
Lagaš
Uruk
Ur
Basra
KUWAIT
Persian Gulf

24/10/2013

SHE WROTE ON CLAY
A Novel

Shirley Graetz

Dear Martin and Joan
Thank you for having me here,
at your Kehila and in your home,
Best,
Shirley Graetz

HADLEY
RILLE
BOOKS

תושר תברק וקריבּ!
מברה שויל.

ISBN-13   978-0-9892631-2-2

Edited by Shauna Roberts and Eric T. Reynolds
Proofread by Deb Sturgess

Published by
Hadley Rille Books
Eric T. Reynolds, Editor/Publisher
PO Box 25466
Overland Park, KS 66225
USA
www.hadleyrillebooks.com
contact@hadleyrillebooks.com

Cover design Heather McDougal.
Cover art "Clay Tablet" © The Schøyen Collection, MS 1713
Cover art "Euphrates River" © Cory Smith.

I dedicate this book to my *Ummu* and *Abu*,
May you live to see many more *naches*.
Love,
Shirley

And in memory of my beloved mentor and Ph.D. advisor
Professor Victor A. Hurowitz,
1948- 2013.

Acknowledgments

This book would never have seen the light of day without the help of many wonderful friends and helpers.

I am grateful for Saray Gutman of Achuzat Bayit Books, an Israeli publishing house. She was one of the first people to hear of my idea for a novel about the *nadītu* women, and she encouraged me a great deal and pointed me in the right direction.

Thanks to Betsy Rosenberg, who helped and encouraged me in the long process of developing the story and special thanks for her great editing of my manuscript.

Thanks to my fellow Assyriologist, Dr. Filip Vukosavović, who advised me on the historical aspects of the book. His excellent insights made the book much better.

Huge thanks to my dear friends Natu, Melanie, Liza, Hadas, Merav, Nurit, and Diane Wohl who read the first raw draft and gave me valuable comments and ideas.

My gratitude to Naomi Graetz, my mother-in-law, who believes in my story and has helped out in so many ways.

As I searched the Internet for novels about the Ancient Near East, I found Shauna Roberts's book, *Like Mayflies in a Stream*, which I read and enjoyed very much. Furthermore, through Roberts, I found Hadley Rille Books. So I am grateful for her writing and also for her comments and suggestions she gave me later on.

I am especially thankful for my publisher, Eric T. Reynolds of Hadley Rille Books. I am lucky to have found him. I thank him for believing in my book and for publishing it.

Last but not least,

To my husband, Rabbi Tzvi Graetz, thank you for having so much patience, for being a wonderful father and a kind and loving man, and for teaching me to see things from a better perspective. When I am with you, there is nothing more I need.

To my three adorable, beautiful, sweet, smart, and energetic children:

Uriah Avshalom,

Ayelet Lucy,

Talya Miriam.

Thank you for being born, for making me a mother. Your presence completes my soul.

In this book, translations of original ancient texts are shown in *italics*.

Chapter 1

"YOUR *UMMU* SENT ME TO FETCH YOU. It's late," said the servant.

"All right, Shima-ahati, I'm coming," Iltani mumbled. Eyes still shut, she heard Shima-ahati climb down from the roof and listened to the familiar morning sounds: *Ummu* ordering the servant and Sin-rēmēni playing with his new puppy downstairs. He had named him Humbaba, a monster from the Gilgamesh story.

In the distance, she heard birds calling, donkeys braying and a rooster crowing. The city of Sippar was coming to life.

Slowly opening her eyes, Iltani stretched her limbs and gazed up at the bright canopy flapping overhead in the morning breeze. She savored this last moment of solitude before starting the day.

With a sigh, she sat up. It was late, and all the family mattresses but hers were stacked against the wall.

During the hot summer months, when the house became stifling, it was lovely to sleep on the roof, but now in the month of Tašîrtu, the nights were sometimes too chilly. Soon the family would sleep downstairs again. As a child, on summer nights, she would sometimes lie awake with her best friend Tabbija, whose family slept on the adjoining rooftop, separated only by a row of mud-bricks. The girls would chatter till the stars fell from the sky, falling asleep long after everyone else. Three years had gone by since Tabbija left for the *gagû*, but soon Iltani would see her again. She was looking forward to rekindling their friendship.

Iltani picked herself up, wound the covers around the poles, and stacked her mattress with the others. Still sleepy, she took a long swallow from the big water jar, splashing her face and neck till the drops trickled down her gown and over her breasts and belly.

Sippar was divided by water-filled canals into various quarters filled with one and two-story houses, temples and courtyards. The sunlight on the water sparkled, gold on blue, and the gleaming white ziggurat where the gods live towered above the city. Iltani stood and gazed around her, thanking Šamaš in her heart for the sights she loved so well.

Wide awake now, and eager to start the day, she thought about the *gagû*. In three months, her new life would begin, the life of her dreams. She would join the honorable class of *nadītu*-women in the prestigious *gagû* of Sippar. As far back as she could remember, *Abu* used to tell her how proud he would be to say his daughter was a *nadītu* and a scribe, "the best female scribe in all of Sippar," he always added. That was what the gods intended for her.

Iltani made her way down to the toilet room behind the stairs and then crossed the courtyard, the heart of the house. All the rooms opened out to the courtyard, and with no street windows, it provided the only light and air. Sunshades made of palm fronds covered the jars and reed mats in the corner. Under one of them, Shima-ahati, the old servant kneeled, husking barley. "Well finally—good morning, Iltani." She greeted her with affection.

"Good morning, Shima-ahati," Iltani replied.

"Iltani? Is that you? Please come here," her mother called.

In the small pantry that led to the cooking room, dried fish and ropes of dates dangled from the ceiling. There were baskets everywhere and pots of all sizes, barley in the large ones on the floor, and on the wooden shelves above them, chick peas, lentils and condiments in medium-size pots, and smaller jars for sesame oil and date syrup.

Iltani walked through to find her mother sitting on a reed mat, grinding the husked barley. More jars stood in the cooking room beside the onion bin and the garlic chains hanging from the wall.

"Good morning, my girl, I trust you slept enough," she said with a hint of good-natured derision.

"I'm sorry I woke so late this morning, *Ummu*, I just couldn't fall asleep last night. Too many thoughts running through my head. I kept thinking about the *gagû* and. . ."

"I know," her mother interrupted. "I felt you tossing and turning beside me on the mattress until very late. I could not sleep either." Iltani shrugged her shoulders in apology.

"Listen, my girl," said *Ummu*, "when you finish eating, I have some errands for you. First, you must go to the storeroom and pick out three lengths of cloth for yourself. You will need more dresses for the *gagû*, and knowing how slow you are with the needle, it may take you a long time to finish. I doubt you'll have time or patience for sewing once you're installed in the *gagû*, at least not at first."

* * *

Iltani's mind wandered to her favorite room—*Abu*'s library—with its welcoming red and brown carpet, and the large wooden chest inlaid with lapis lazuli and golden stripes, inscribed with the proverb: "*A scribe whose hand competes with his mouth—he indeed is a scribe.*" Her father had received the chest as a wedding gift from his wealthy family.

Iltani dreamed of one day owning such a chest, with plenty of space for reeds and clay. Behind the chest was an alcove with three shelves of clay tablets in various sizes inscribed with lexical lists, stories, poems, letters and contracts.

As a child, Iltani had liked to cuddle up on a cushion in the corner and watch *Abu* at work, sometimes for hours,

13

intoxicated by the smell of moist clay. Her esteem for her *Abu* was boundless, and there was no one she loved more. He inspired in her a passion for clay tablets, as he would read poems and myths aloud to her, discussing them afterward. Their lessons together were sacred times for both of them.

"Come eat, we'll choose the cloth later." *Ummu* forced Iltani out of her reverie. "And, after that, take Sin-rēmēni with you to buy some fresh fish. We've had none for some time."

Eat, choose fabrics, buy fish—Iltani repeated as she crossed the courtyard.

On her way back through the pantry, she opened the reed hamper, untied the sack inside, and pulled out a lump of dough. Iltani began to knead it.

"Don't forget to knot the string and close the lid," her mother hollered from the cooking room. "Two days ago, someone forgot to tie it properly, and you do not want to know what I found there in the evening."

Her mother made the finest dough and her bread always came out sweet and fluffy because of the sesame oil, the spices and fig juice she added to the usual mix of flour, salt and water. Iltani spread the flattened dough over the oven dome in the courtyard and went back for the date honey, chick peas and dried figs. She ate cross-legged on the reed mat beside the old servant Shima-ahati and watched her rolling the barley between her palms with smooth, rhythmical movements to separate it from the husk.

"Ah, I shall miss you," Shima-ahati sighed. "I remember how I nursed you, and what a comfort it was after the loss of my stillborn infant. And how funny you were as a little girl running after your father with a piece of clay, forever entreating, '*Abu*, do you have time to teach me now?' You are like a daughter to me. What will I do when you are gone? Who will make me laugh?" she asked accusingly.

14

Iltani did not feel like listening to her just then. She knew that Shima-ahati disapproved of her entering the *gagû*. She had said so on every possible occasion.

"Don't be sad, I will be allowed home visits in two years, and you still have Sin-rēmēni who needs you as much as I did," said Iltani.

But the servant was still baffled—why was Iltani so happy, how could she make such a sacrifice—no husband, no children, no family of her own? Again, she asked the same questions.

"Please, will you help me find the fabric trunk in the storeroom?" Iltani said, changing the subject.

The servant lit two lamps from the fire. To enter the darkened storeroom, they had to pass through the main room of the house where the family slept when it got too cold on the roof. Sometimes *Ummu* and *Abu* would hang a curtain around their mattresses, and in the morning, all mattresses were stacked in the corner and covered with cloth. On rainy winter days, they used the main room instead of the courtyard for all their activities, especially to welcome guests.

Iltani and Shima-ahati entered the storeroom behind the wooden door. In the dim light of the lamps, Iltani found the trunk and dragged it out to the main room, where she began to sort through it. She chose three lengths of cloth, two of rather coarse wool, but dyed a lovely reddish-brown, and one soft, cream-colored weave with purple stripes.

She wanted to look agreeable on her first day at the *gagû*, to make a pleasant impression on her aunt and the other *nadītu*, daughters of priests, army chiefs, wealthy merchants, scribes, judges, and the King's own sister, the Princess. Aside from her aunt, the only other person Iltani knew there was her childhood friend, Tabbija. She was eager to see her best friend again and continue their friendship, just as it was before Tabbija had left for the *gagû*.

15

They returned the trunk to the storeroom and Iltani hurried out to show *Ummu* the fabrics she had chosen. *Ummu* was about to mix ingredients for the evening meal, having finished grinding the barley. "Oh yes, these will do quite nicely," she said, praising Iltani's good taste. "Now will you take Sin-rēmēni to buy fish?"

"Iltani, are you there?" *Abu* called on his return from morning offerings to Nabû- god of the scribes.

"I must speak with *Abu* first, then I will go," Iltani said, running out to the courtyard where she jumped into her father's arms, forgetting she was not a child anymore.

"I have a small gift for you," he said, hugging her with a mysterious smile.

"What is it?" she asked, filled with excitement.

"Come, let's go into our É-DUBBA."

* * *

The É-DUBBA—the school was what *Abu* called the library when he occasionally taught her the basics of reading and writing.

Of his four children, two boys and two girls, the eldest Marduk-ili had become a scribe. Gifted and successful, nimble with the reed-stylus, his memory was as retentive as Iltani's. But unlike her, he was indifferent to content. It mattered little to him whether he was inscribing a prayer to the gods or a sales contract, so long as his work was flawless.

Abu observed Iltani's growing interest in the scribal arts from an early age. Then and there he decided to groom his daughter to become a *nadītu* and a scribe. It was a great honor to be accepted into the *gagû* of Sippar, and he did everything in his power to make Iltani choose that path for herself. He would describe the grandeur of the *gagû* and teach her just enough to make her want to learn more. He promised that once she became a *nadītu*, she would learn the skills of a real scribe.

"Here is the gift. I have paid a *nadītu* by the name of Amat-Mamu to teach you in the *gagû*. She is said to be a rigorous teacher, but I have no doubt that she will instruct you well. From her, you will learn everything it takes to become a scribe. And this is the agreement I signed with her yesterday. She is to give you reading and writing lessons, and to take you along with her when she writes for clients. In payment, she will receive three pieces of silver, two lengths of cloth a year, and rations of oil and barley. Here, you see?" *Abu* handed her the clay tablet to read.

Iltani held it carefully to the light streaming in from the courtyard and studied the clusters of signs that slowly turned into words and phrases. She was only able to make out a few signs.

"Thank you, *Abu*," she said, hugging him enthusiastically.

"You will be proud of me, I promise. And what are those other tablets?"

"Ah, those are the inheritance tablets you will receive when you enter the *gagû*. . ." He was about to explain the procedure, when Shima-ahati announced the arrival of two visitors.

"By Nabû—I nearly forgot, I promised to write a letter for a client."

"I will bring out some beer for the guests and a tray of figs. May I watch? Please, *Abu*!"

"Perhaps. I will decide when I meet the client," he said.

* * *

The servant led the two men into the library and Iltani hurried to the pantry. She noticed that one of the men was actually a curly red-haired youth not much older than she was. As she was arranging the dried figs and dates on the tray with the red tassels, *Ummu* strode in and asked impatiently, about the fish and the whereabouts of Sin-rēmēni.

Iltani felt as though she had been caught in some mischievous act and sweetened her tone. "*Ummu*, let me just offer some refreshments to the guests, and after that, I'll take Sin-rēmēni to buy fish. I promise."

Ummu shrugged her shoulders. "I know you will not budge until you have watched your *Abu* write the document. Fine, then," she replied. "Go as soon as the guests leave."

Back in the library, Iltani saw that her *Abu* was talking to the older man while the youth examined a tablet on the shelf. Father and son were both finely dressed, and the older man's tunic had a lapis lazuli clasp.

"This is my daughter Iltani who will be entering the *gagû* soon," *Abu* introduced her proudly.

"And this is my son Marduk-mušallim," replied the older man. "He studies at the É-DUBBA of Babylon."

"Iltani, perhaps you would like to take Marduk-mušallim up to the roof? There's a splendid view of the ziggurat from there. The two of you can join us later," he added, in a tone that meant it would be useless to protest. Iltani did not want to leave, but she trusted that *Abu* had good reasons not to let her stay. Instead she would be a good hostess to that young man.

As they climbed to the roof, Iltani examined him. This Marduk-mušallim was tall and slender, with bright red curls that bounced whenever he moved. She found them enchanting.

* * *

Downstairs, *Abu* took a large piece of clay out of the wooden chest and kneaded it until it was soft enough to mold into a tablet. He beckoned the man to sit down on a cushion beside him.

"What are we writing today?" he asked when the tablet was prepared.

"Family quarrels over inheritances are proverbial, and city laws are so diverse, the courts are always full and my wages assured," the client said, grinning.

"And what is your function in the court?"

"I am in charge of trial witnesses: locating them, making sure they arrive on time, especially those with physical difficulties. In most cases, they come willingly, so there is no need to send an escort of guards. Only when they balk at appearing in the courts, we have to bring them in by force. But what I need to write today concerns a private matter. You know, because of my position in the court, people often approach me with legal questions or ask me to represent them before the authorities. If I can, if I have time, I am glad to help, as in this case, where the petitioner is the daughter of an old friend who died many years ago, and I have been her guardian ever since. Her elder sister, has taken a larger share of the inheritance."

"Is that not against the law?" asked Iltani's father, trying to recall the laws he learned as a youth in the É-DUBBA.

"The laws of Sippar are different from the laws of the south where the two sisters grew up. There the elder child receives a larger portion of the inheritance. But since the younger sister now lives in Sippar, she is claiming an equal share. The younger sister approached the court asking for a trial and I am helping her."

The two men set to work, the client dictating his letter word by word, and *Abu* pressing the stylus into the moist clay, stringing signs into phrases.

* * *

On the roof, Iltani and Marduk-mušallim gazed out at the view. "Sippar is a beautiful city," he said, breaking the silence. "Much bigger than I thought, though it does not compare to Babylon."

"I have never been to Babylon, but I am sure I will go one day," said Iltani. "Tell me, Marduk-mušallim, what is it like at the É-DUBBA?"

The boy was unaccustomed to talking to girls about school life. The girls he knew would usually giggle and whisper whenever he was around, making comments about the color of his hair.

19

"Well to be honest," he said sheepishly, "I can't wait to leave the É-DUBBA and start working. I've been a pupil since the age of nine, so I've just about had enough," he laughed with a toss of his red curls.

"I intend to become a scribe. *Abu* has taught me how to read and write a little, but not the É-DUBBA way, I'm sure," Iltani said.

"But female scribes are a rarity," he said. "Like Sargon's daughter, for instance. At the É-DUBBA, we had to memorize the hymns she composed to the goddess Inanna, like this one:

> *"Lady Inanna, shining with splendor,*
> *May your heart be moved for me.*
> *In deeds supreme you reign supreme*
> *Eternally your praises ring*
> *With sweet adoration, my Lady."*

"So why do you wish to learn how to read and write?" Marduk-mušallim asked.

"I wish to learn because I like to learn!" Iltani said proudly, holding her head high. "My memory is good, as good as my brother's and he is a scribe. Since there are no É-DUBBA's for girls and my father always told me I have the gift to become a scribe, it was decided that I would enter the *gagû*, and there I will study with a famous *nadītu* scribe. And one day, with the help of the gods, I too will be a scribe. Girls can be scribes too."

Surprised by her sharp tone, yet impressed by her confidence and directness, the boy decided it would be best to answer her questions rather than ask any more of his own.

He searched for a way to describe his world: "At the É-DUBBA you study from dawn to dusk. In the first year, the big brother teaches you how to make a reed stylus and wedge the signs in the clay. . ."

"Who is the big brother?" Iltani said, interrupting him.

"At my É-DUBBA, the 'big-brother' is a more advanced pupil, who teaches the young beginners. He writes a copy-tablet for them, examines their work, and listens to their recitation from memory. Once a student reaches a high enough level, he learns with different tutors—scribes for calculation, experts on Sumerian, and my personal favorite," he added dryly, "'the whip-master' whose task it is to oversee our studies. Some whip-masters take pleasure in flogging while others merely threaten. . . But no one escapes them. And the. . ." He wanted to add something, but was interrupted by a call from downstairs.

Marduk-mušallim wished there had been more time to talk, but Iltani's *Abu* summoned them. He liked this strange, beautiful girl. She was of average height and very slender with wavy dark brown hair that underlined her nearly-black eyes. But her most prominent feature was the sweet dimple that appeared whenever she smiled, making her whole face glow. A more confident youth might have paid her compliments, but Marduk-mušallim was too shy.

They entered the library in time to hear Iltani's *Abu* read aloud from the end of the letter.

"*. . .When I arrive, I will escort you to the judges of Sippar. They will examine your case, approach the palace and compensate you for your losses. Different inheritance laws for younger and older offspring do not exist in Sippar.*"

The older client wrapped the tablet carefully in a cloth and paid Iltani's *Abu*.

"May Šamaš keep you safe in your new life at the *gagú*," he said to Iltani.

Marduk-mušallim smiled bashfully: "I wish you good fortune in your studies," he said in parting, before the servant escorted them out to the street.

* * *

21

"Iltani, I too must go now, I have a contract to write for a merchant in the *kārum*—the merchant's quarter," said *Abu*. He left, hurrying out, bidding farewell to his youngest child, Sin-rēmēni, who was waiting in the doorway to the courtyard with his drowsy brown puppy, Humbaba.

Iltani followed her *Abu* into the court.

"Let's go, little brother," Iltani said to Sin-rēmēni. "Who knows what interesting things we may see on our trip to the fishmonger."

Chapter 2

"I CAN'T BREATHE. The stench is everywhere . . . baaaa. . ."
Sin-rēmēni grimaced, holding his breath as long as he could.

"Come now, Sin-rēmēni, it's only fish, just breathe through your mouth. Wait till *Ummu* grills it on the embers and we have it for our evening meal with cress and barley porridge," Iltani said as they walked through the *kārum*, where burly fishermen peddled their wares. The strong smell of fish did not disturb her. It was their dead eyes. In the lane ahead, two grey cats were picking at a carp, one tearing pieces of flesh off the spine while the other licked the eye sockets clean. Iltani turned away in disgust, grasping Sin-rēmēni's hand.

Peddlers sat outside their homes with lengths of cloth dyed brown, red, ochre and indigo, folded in piles or spread out before them. The fabrics were of different texture and quality, finely-spun, knotted or coarsely woven with animal hair. Behind them were piles of reed baskets and braided palm-leaf mats. Boisterous cries filled the crowded lanes and Sin-rēmēni clasped Iltani's hand more tightly.

The fishmongers' stalls were just ahead. The daily river catch went first to the palace and temples and the remains were sold to ordinary people. Whenever King Hammurabi visited the city, or before a temple feast was held, the stalls stood empty. But today there were plenty of fresh-looking fish spread out on mats covered with cool, damp cloths. Glassy fish-eyes stared back at Iltani and Sin-rēmēni.

"I want three of these," she told the fishmonger as soon as he was free. He wrapped three of the larger fish in a wet cloth and placed them in her basket. "Your *Ummu* will be pleased," he said, weighing out the pile of barley she paid him in exchange.

"Please, Iltani, let's run down to the river before we go home," begged the lively eight-year-old, eager to watch the boats and the fishermen.

"All right, since we're so close to the river, but we have to get the fish home to *Ummu* before it spoils."

They pressed through the crowd until they reached the city gate on the banks of the Euphrates. Long lines of people and donkeys laden with goods stirred up the dust and sand. Outside the gate stood a group of the King's soldiers questioning a tanner about the pile of freshly stripped hides on his two-wheeled donkey cart. Trying to avoid the stench of the leather, they quickly called a scribe over to read the tanner's slate to them. Iltani imagined some of the wedge-like symbols as the scribe read them out. The words seemed to confirm what he had said, so the soldiers, satisfied, moved aside to let him pass.

Sin-rēmēni pulled his sister in the direction of the river, thrilled at the sight of a boat in the distance: "Look, look Iltani!" he exclaimed, pointing south. "A hauler tied to the pier. What are those men loading onto it?"

Iltani saw a long flat-bottomed boat with dark red stripes floating gracefully on the green-mud colored water. "It's the royal barge," said Iltani with awe, wondering what freight it was carrying into the city. Perhaps something special for the *gagû*?

"Iltani—look—over there!" Sin-rēmēni pointed. He was waving at three men in the river clutching inflated animal bladders to keep afloat. One of the men held a net spread half way across the river, while the other two dived in and out of the water using trawls tied to a stick.

Further down the river, Iltani caught sight of a group of women among the reeds on the bank, washing clothes. A tall muscular fisherman was eyeing one of the young girls.

When a young girl leaned over and whispered something to the group of women, something Iltani couldn't hear, they all laughed mirthfully. Iltani could only guess what the joke was about. The girl, like Iltani, was of marriageable age: only Iltani was entering the *gagû*, she would never be with a man, never have a husband. Still, she knew about the ways of men and women, from bawdy ballads and wedding songs and from sleeping on the roof, where there was much to see and hear at night, and the rest to imagine.

But her destiny was to be different, special, as her father told her so many times; she was to become a scribe, not a mother or wife. She was pleased with the path the gods had chosen for her.

She gazed at the river flowing gently southward to Babylon, the city of King Hammurabi and the *Ésagila* temple of the god Marduk. "One day I will see it in all its splendor," she mused.

"Come, Sin-rēmēni, it's getting late," Iltani said, tugging his hand. "We have to bring the fish home to *Ummu*." She stroked her brother's hair as they headed home.

* * *

By the time Sin-rēmēni was born, Iltani's older brother Marduk-ili had become a practiced scribe, and moved to Sippar-Amnanum, another quarter of greater Sippar, with a wife and family of his own. Then Iltani's big sister Šamhat had married and moved to her husband's city, Nippur. Iltani, nine years old when Sin-rēmēni was born, felt an illimitable tenderness toward him, and it was she, not *Ummu*, who had bathed him, held him, played with him constantly and nursed him back to health when he was ill. She was sometimes more of a mother to him than a sister, an arrangement that suited everyone.

It should have been a short walk home but the sight of the temple as they passed late in the morning was so riveting for Sin-rēmēni, that Iltani slowed her pace. Sin-rēmēni's curiosity fed her joy in explaining things and they sat down together under a shady plane tree to watch passersby on their way to the grand court of the Šamaš-temple, the Ziggurat and the surrounding domiciles and storehouses.

Before them was a staircase that led to a large wooden gate, decorated with a spiky crown. Crowds bearing offerings ascended and descended the stairs to the main court.

"Can we go in, just to look?" pleaded Sin-rēmēni.

"Without an offering?" said Iltani, alarmed at the thought of entering the temple—where the god lived—without even a small sacrifice. "Well, all right," she relented, "we'll walk up the stairs and peek in through the gate, but that's all."

Through the gate, they glimpsed the spacious courtyard filled with worshippers entering and leaving the various chambers. A small group of people shouted and gesticulated before the presiding judge of the day who sat on a stone chair. Opposite the gate, on the other side of the courtyard stood the white ziggurat that towered over the temple complex and the city. At the very top was the abode of Šamaš and his family of deities, which only the King, the high-priest and the high-priestess were allowed to enter.

To the left, on the other side of the courtyard, another large gate in the wall opened to a smaller courtyard. This smaller complex included the chambers of the high-priest, storerooms, and most importantly, the temple of Šamaš and statue of the god, only seen by the temple priests. The worshipers had to be satisfied with the emblem of the god as they made their offerings.

"You see that small gate to the right of the ziggurat?" Iltani said, pointing in the direction of the wall. "That gate connects directly to the *gagû*. Through it I will enter the temple when I bring my offerings," she said enthusiastically. Sin-rēmēni's eyes widened with excitement, as he took a closer look at the ziggurat gleaming in the morning sun.

Iltani was also giddy. The wall to the right of the ziggurat was low enough to afford a view of the flat roofs of the *gagû* compound, but high enough to hide the people inside. These walls would soon surround her, revealing and concealing her new life.

"Come Sin-rēmēni! If we don't leave now, the fish will spoil!" They quickly skipped down the stairs. But as they passed a small shrine to Nabû, god of the scribes, Iltani stopped a moment to whisper a prayer. Sin-rēmēni watched her earnestly, babbling about the royal barge and life along the river. Iltani knew that today her little brother wished to become a fisherman, tomorrow no doubt he would change his mind. Though she was sure that *Abu* wanted him to be a scribe.

They crossed the wooden bridge over the drinking water canal. Sometimes boys would jump over it for sport or even push each other off into the canal, even though fouling the water was an offense punishable by a heavy fine. The walls of the canal were freshly plastered twice a year to keep the water clear, and shimmering in the sunlight. Negligence over the canals was a grievous sin punishable by the gods.

* * *

Home was only a few steps away. Iltani ran to her mother with the basket of fish and hurried out to help Shima-ahati grind barley for the evening bread. They squatted on a mat together in the courtyard, shaking the flour into a large pannier.

Sin-rēmēni rested his head on Iltani's shoulder. "I will miss you very much, when you go," he said.

Iltani felt a sharp pang. She would miss him too, very much.

"I promise I will visit you as often as possible and. . ." she started to say, but was interrupted by an angry shout from the cooking room: "Sin-rēmēni!!! Come here and clean up after your dog!" Sin-rēmēni ran off, ending the beginning of a gloomy conversation. Iltani felt both saddened and relieved.

* * *

Ummu finished hanging fish to dry over the fire. A large pot filled with lentils, garlic, onions, and barley mixed with spices simmered in the clay oven. The porridge would be cooked in time for dinner and the fish would be ready to grill on the embers.

Then Iltani's mother set off for the potter's house. Iltani needed a number of articles for the *gagû*, and today she would buy her pottery wares. Sin-rēmēni promised to behave himself if she would take him along, and *Ummu*, feeling guilty for neglecting him amidst all the preparations, happily consented.

"May Šamaš keep you in good health. What can I do for my lady?" the potter said, greeting *Ummu*. He was a husky, fair-skinned man with a booming voice and wild blue eyes that made him stand out among his dark-eyed neighbors. Still, he was popular with women, and not merely because of his blue-eyed charms. He was an exceptional potter as well.

"I would like to buy a jug and a few small oil-lamps for my daughter," said *Ummu* with a smile.

"Plain or painted? I have some lovely colorful ones here, in the latest style," he said, enticing her, knowing his customers.

"Oh yes, the painted ones," she said, and the potter displayed his different wares. "What pleasing colors!" *Ummu* complemented him.

"Thank you. May Šamaš bless you! I use only the finest clay and all my wares are thick and strong but no less lovely for that."

Ummu chose two smaller lamps for Iltani, and one medium size jug, in shades of blue with delicate, gold stripes with tiny shimmering stones imbedded near the lip.

Meanwhile Sin-rēmēni glanced around the courtyard, much smaller than their courtyard at home, with only one entrance to a room. Pots and clay shards were scattered everywhere near the remains of a large kiln.

He began to explore the wares on display; to his eye, the decorations on the vessels looked much the same, though they were of different shapes and sizes. And then, peeking out from behind a large pot, he spotted one with painted figures. When he picked it up and looked it over, he quickly recognized the two figures, Gilgamesh and his friend Enkidu pursuing the monster Humbaba in the cedar forest. Iltani used to tell him Gilgamesh stories at night when she put him to bed.

"*Ummu*, could I have this one? Please?" He brought the pot to his mother.

"Hah!" said the potter, "do you know who those three are?"

"Yes, my sister Iltani told me the Gilgamesh stories," he answered, proudly. "I have named my dog Humbaba."

"Well, some people call me Humbaba, behind my back, as well," he said without the faintest trace of anger, "because I am so big of course, and because of my wild hair." He laughed heartily. "You're in luck, my boy. An É-DUBBA-master from Babylon ordered this pot for his class and later he cancelled the order though he had already paid for it. I will give it to you as a present," he said and smiled at *Ummu*, who paid him for the wares she had chosen. Sin-rēmēni held his precious new possession to his heart.

Ummu could not help adding with pride: "My daughter is entering the *gagû* in a few weeks."

"May the gods bless her, and come back if you need more bowls, pots, lamps, anything at all," he called after them as they left.

The potter watched them walk away. He often sold wares to *nadītu* women and heard their complaints. By law, a

29

nadītu's father bore the responsibility for providing her with food and raiment. If he died, the responsibility fell to her brothers. Often this led to feuds and lawsuits. But the potter had little sympathy for their grievances. Compared to other women they enjoyed a high status, with no troubles, no birthing pains. And frequently their situation only improved with the years, as some of them became successful business women.

* * *

"Thank you *Ummu*," Iltani said after the evening meal, "it was delicious, especially the fish."

"Thank you, *Ummu*," echoed Sin-rēmēni. "May Iltani and I go look at my present now?"

"Yes, go," *Ummu* answered. Iltani and Sin-rēmēni ran up to the roof to make their beds and look at the Gilgamesh pot.

Ummu and *Abu* stayed by the fire, discussing their day.

"Last week when I met with your sister to talk about Iltani's adoption, she looked distressingly pale. I think Amat-Šamaš may be ill. I'm worried about her," *Abu* said.

"I will pray for her health. I noticed it too when I met her a month ago," *Ummu* said.

* * *

Abu gazed up at the first stars in the evening sky. Would his sister-in-law be able to ease Iltani's transition into her new life in the *gagû*? He was proud of her becoming a *nadītu*; he felt honored. However, would she learn fast enough how to look out for herself? He sat very still in the fast-fading light and tried not to fear for her. At length, he promised his personal god to offer a double portion next morning at the temple if he would intercede with Šamaš and Aja, patrons of the *gagû*, to ensure his daughter's happiness.

Chapter 3

"MY LORD, THE BUILDERS MUST BE PAID. They have been working for over two weeks now without wages. I gave my word that we would settle with them," said the older priest, bowing deferentially to the UGULA, Rapaš-ṣilli-Ea, overseer of the *nadītu.*

As he stood up again, he could not help noticing all the changes in Rapaš-ṣilli-Ea's chamber. The room, a model of simplicity in the days of the previous UGULA, who had been a modest and devoted priest, was now full of costly tables inlaid with ivory and sumptuous, finely knotted carpets. The priest, by now the oldest ministrant of the god Šamaš, disliked this haughty and corrupt overseer. How had the man risen to such a lofty position? Anyone could see that he lacked the priestly virtues expected of an UGULA.

"I'm quite certain that we don't have enough barley to pay them right now. Why don't you ask the accountant-scribe?"

The old priest was taken aback by the UGULA's answer. They had both been present at the temple assembly when King Hammurabi dispensed silver and barley to pay for the repairs of the *gagû* walls, and he distinctly remembered hearing this UGULA promise to see the task completed. Had the man no shame? How could he lie so brazenly?

"Is that all? I am busy now," said the UGULA crossly, indicating that he was not to be disturbed again. "When you leave, have my secretary come in," he ordered the old priest.

The old priest felt powerless. He excused himself and left with a heavy heart. I see dark clouds over the *gagû*, he thought as he walked along. But what can I do? Nothing. Perhaps we displeased the god Šamaš in some way and in punishment, he sent this UGULA.

Outside the UGULA's chamber, several priests were engaged in lively conversation. The old priest interrupted them with the UGULA's message. The secretary hurried in.

As the old priest made his way through the *gagû* compound, he saw three women approach. His eyesight was failing so that only as they came nearer did he recognize the Princess, Hammurabi's sister, with her maidservant and a young *nadītu* in attendance. The old priest bowed to the Princess, who wore a grave expression as they passed. He looked up at the sky again, wondering if this was a further bad omen from the god Šamaš.

* * *

The women marched up to the UGULA's door, and the party of priests scattered as the Princess stormed through with her two attendants, interrupting the UGULA's orders to his secretary.

"Honorable Princess," said the UGULA in surprise. "May Šamaš and Aja keep you in good health forever. What can your loyal servant do for you today?" He was well aware of the Princess' aversion to him. Her coming here could only mean trouble.

"Rapaš-ṣilli-Ea, as UGULA of the *gagû*, you are required to intercede whenever a *nadītu* of Šamaš is wronged. Such is the case of Tabbija, the young *nadītu* before you."

"But of course, Princess," he replied. He cared nothing about this girl, Tabbija, but would go through the motions. The Princess was King Hammurabi's sister after all, and a most influential woman in her own right. He would have to play along and give her what she wanted.

"Well then, tell me, Tabbija, what happened?" Rapaš-ṣilli-Ea continued.

Tabbija sought the Princess' eyes for reassurance and began to explain to the UGULA: "My most valuable slave, Liwira-ana-ilim, has been taken into military service by the river governor. Liwira-ana-ilim was born to the slave of my deceased aunt, and has been in our family ever since. The commander had no right to conscript him. He is young, still a youth, and he manages my land and crops. He is a most loyal slave and. . ." She stopped talking and bit her lip. Tears appeared in her eyes.

"On what grounds did the river governor conscript him?" asked the UGULA.

Seeing that Tabbija was distraught, the Princess interposed with more information about the slave's legal status. Furthermore, she warned the UGULA, Tabbija would approach the King himself if he did not settle the affair at once.

The UGULA was in a tight spot. The river governor happened to be an old friend of his, yet the law was clearly against him. In truth, he had no right to conscript the young *nadītu*'s slave. To appease the Princess, he would have to reprimand his friend in all severity. Still, he could intimate that he was doing so against his will, for otherwise the *nadītu* would turn to the King, with the help of the Princess.

Tabbija held her breath as he called the scribe in and began to dictate a letter:

"To the governor of the river say: thus says Rapaš-ṣilli-Ea (the UGULA).

May Šamaš and Marduk keep you in good health!

Why did you detain Liwira-ana-ilim, the slave of a nadītu of Šamaš?

He is not a citizen of Sippar, he is not the son of a free man, but a slave of a nadītu of Šamaš. Release him at once, lest the nadītu of

Šamaš approach the King for help. Why have you inscribed him for military service? The gagû may not be plundered!"

After the scribe read the letter back aloud, the Princess turned to the UGULA:

"I expect you to keep me informed about this. A few weeks should be enough time to settle the matter. See to it that this *nadītu* has no reason to turn to the King. Thank you for your assistance," she said curtly and turned to leave with her servant and Tabbija.

When the UGULA was sure they were out of earshot, he dismissed his scribe and then spit out his fury with a curse at the woman who had just humiliated him in public. Then he cursed the river governor for putting him in this nasty predicament. He cared nothing about the young *nadītu* and her slave. All he could think about was the fact that the Princess had wasted his time on such a trivial matter. He needed to clear his mind—a visit to the inn would do just that. The mistress of the inn would know exactly what and whom to dish up for him. He took off his fine cotton gown with the gold stripes and threw on a light woolen tunic held by a shoulder brooch. Himself again, he left his chamber and walked in direction of the *kārum*. The inn there was one of the best in Sippar and he was a regular patron. He would take care of the other business later. In the distance, he discerned the Princess and the young *nadītu* engaged in conversation and he turned down a side path to avoid them.

* * *

"I must hear of it as soon as Liwira-ana-ilim is released, Tabbija," said the Princess, and continued on her way to the *Šamaš* temple with an offering.

Tabbija felt utterly wretched. Liwira-ana-ilim was far more to her than a loyal slave who managed her fields; they had grown up together.

Tabbija had almost reached her residence when she saw Amat-Šamaš, the older *nadītu* she knew as the aunt of her childhood friend, Iltani. Though she was not in the mood to speak to anyone, she wanted news of Iltani, so she approached Amat-Šamaš.

"May Aja and Šamaš keep you in good health! How is Iltani? I have heard nothing from her since I entered the *gagû*," Tabbija said.

"May Aja keep you healthy. How do you know Iltani?" Amat-Šamaš asked.

"We were neighbors and friends, though I am a few years older," she said.

"Well, you and Iltani will very soon be able to resume your friendship, as she is coming to the *gagû*."

"Soon—truly?" Tabbija asked with a flickering of joy on her eyes. "Please send her my affectionate regards." She bid farewell to Amat-Šamaš and walked on.

* * *

Iltani is coming to live with me, Amat-Šamaš thought uneasily as she continued to walk. Her secure routine was about to change. Long-suppressed memories would pierce the shell she had maintained for as long as she could remember. It was beginning to crack now, little by little, as Iltani's arrival drew near. And then a painful memory pierced her to the heart. That room . . . long, long ago.

"Pardon me, but are you going in?" A man's voice brought Amat-Šamaš back to the present. She had entered the Šamaš-temple, unaware.

"Yes, I have brought my offering," she told the priest as through a fog.

"Well then, you will have to hurry—we are about to close the gates."

Amat-Šamaš was confused. How and why had those memories re-surfaced after all this time? But of course, she knew the reason only too well. It was Iltani.

She watched the priest and the other *nadītu* and the last of the worshippers entering the hall where the emblem of Šamaš stood. Amat-Šamaš followed them reverently. The gleaming walls and high ceiling offered a strong contrast to the golden emblem of the god. On it was a relief of Šamaš wearing a conical crown.

Baskets of grains, fruits and vegetables sat on tables. A goat and two sheep were tethered to a ring in the wall.

Amat-Šamaš drew closer, as close as permitted, and gazed at the emblem. For the first time in years, she felt something besides her usual indifference. Love, happiness, doubt—these Amat-Šamaš had locked away, but one strong emotion had escaped now and forced its way into her consciousness: anger. So much anger, that she balled her hands forcefully into fists as she knelt, praying to the god.

"Šamaš, beloved master, shine your light upon this loyal servant forever," she whispered. "The anger you find in me, omniscient god, is a danger to the only family I know. Help me, please. Remove it from my heart," she prayed, trembling as she pronounced the words. Without any warning, another memory broke through her shield till she groaned in pain.

The other worshippers stared and a priest approached her and asked gently if she needed help. Amat-Šamaš composed herself. She desperately wanted to get home. She whispered her thanks to the priest, placed her offering on the table with the others, and hurried back to the *gagû*, still shaken and lost.

Safe in her room again, she called her servant and ordered her to warm up some water for washing, and meanwhile she poured herself a cup of beer. She had to think. The secret she had guarded all these years would no longer be safe, now that Iltani was coming.

Chapter 4

"THE FEAST IS SUMPTUOUS! *Ummu* must have toiled for days," said Šamhat, Iltani's older sister, who came from Nippur with all her family for the special event.

"*Ummu* and the additional servants she hired all worked from dawn till dusk," Iltani told her.

"Three kinds of bread—imagine that! We only had two at my wedding feast," Šamhat said, winking at Iltani. "Iltani, what a magnificent occasion. May Šamaš bless you and grant you happiness all your life," she added.

The courtyard was crowded with friends and relations helping themselves from the trays of plentiful food. Servants refilled their cups with brown beer or ruby pomegranate juice. Some of the younger cousins scurried up and down the stairway to the roof, screaming and laughing. Oil lamps and torches had been spaced around the courtyard, ready to light when the sun set. The air rang with the voices of the guests and the sweet, soft music of the lyre.

"By your leave, my friends, I would like to say a few words," said *Abu*, clapping his hands for attention.

"This is a most fortunate day for us and especially for our daughter Iltani. The gods have truly blessed this family, and today, in gratitude for our good fortune, we bring a special offering to the temple of Šamaš. Iltani, dear daughter," he searched the crowd for her face. "I am proud that you have been accepted to enter the *gagû*; you bring great honor to this family. I am certain you will fulfill your destiny of becoming an exceptional scribe and find happiness and joy in your future life. May Šamaš and Aja keep you healthy forever."

"May Šamaš and Aja keep you healthy forever," cheers rang from all directions.

"And now I will present you with a gift," continued *Abu*, signaling the servants to carry it out. "It is something you will need when you become a scribe, a wooden chest for storing clay and reeds and tablets. May the joys you find in learning and writing never diminish."

The musician began to play a fast rhythmical tune on the lyre, to the accompaniment of drums. The men danced around Iltani and her father, clapping and singing to the music, and the women danced around the circle of men. Iltani, overwhelmed, escaped the whirling rings and watched from the side. She felt uncomfortable with all the commotion just for her. After a while, the music slowed down and the servants brought out jugs of refreshing fig juice and a platter of roasted locusts, a luxurious treat no one could resist.

* * *

"Look at the ivory inlay on that chest," Iltani overheard one of her neighbors say. "It must have cost a fortune. And the cornelian beading. What craftsmanship."

"The exquisite quality of the wood," said his wife. "A very generous gift."

"Yes indeed, but a poor substitute for a family and children. Wouldn't you agree?" asked the man.

"The girl's path has been chosen for her, and she seems to keenly want it as well. Let us hope she will be happy. Some women find contentment without husband and children," his wife said.

"That may be, but what if she regrets that life one day and wishes she had taken a different path? What then? Even if she could leave the *gagû*, it may be too late for her to have children," said the young neighbor, tenderly caressing the belly of his wife, heavy with child.

* * *

The sun had almost set by the time Amat-Šamaš called Iltani and *Ummu* to her side.

"Here," she said, handing them each a length of cloth. "These are for you."

Ummu's eyes grew wide with surprise as she examined the delicate blue weave with the ochre stripes, and Iltani's brightly painted cotton. "Thank you, Amat-Šamaš, these are very fine," she said.

"Yes, thank you, dear aunt," Iltani added.

"I must go now, but I will see you in the *gagû*," she replied abruptly, and left.

"I had not expected such a gift from my sister. The fabrics must have been quite costly," Iltani's mother whispered to her daughter.

Iltani watched her aunt disappear down the path with her servant and wondered how it would be to live with this near stranger. She seemed so distant, so cold. Would Amat-Šamaš learn to like her?

"*Ummu*, was Amat-Šamaš always like this?" Iltani asked. "I mean she is your sister. What was she like when you were growing up?"

"She left when I was just an infant. Strangely, my parents seldom spoke about her. I remember seeing her once when I was about ten, as she came for a visit. She brought me some fine cloth, but barely said a word to me. The night she stayed with us, I heard her quarrelling loudly with my parents.

"I never told you this, but when I was about seventeen, Amat-Šamaš offered me a large dowry so I would marry a high ranking husband, a much larger dowry than my parents could ever afford. But there was one condition: I would come to live in Sippar and she would find me the right suitor. I was reluctant at first, but my *Ummu* persuaded me and I agreed to go. This was my only way out of a life of servitude and poverty," she said. "Once I married your *Abu*, a wonderful man, thanks to Amat-Šamaš, I rarely heard from her, though we both live in Sippar. She behaved coldly when I asked to see her and seemed indifferent to our family. So I left it at that. I was grateful and happy to raise you and your brothers and sisters, my beautiful children."

"Well, I hope we will get along," Iltani said with a slight worry.

The servants began to clear the courtyard as more and more of the guests departed. Those who lived far away stayed overnight, so mattresses and blankets had been obtained for them and arranged in the big room. Iltani lay down beside Sin-rēmēni who was fast asleep. She hugged him tightly. She had not shared her true feelings with anyone, the excitement mixed with fears and the pain of leaving her family.

* * *

Two days after Iltani's feast, Amat-Šamaš took her morning *piqittu*-offering to the Šamaš-temple. Seeing Iltani with her mother had brought back agonizing memories of herself as a young girl, living at home long before her days in the *gagû*. Forget, forget, she told herself, but how?

When the sun reached its zenith, her head began to throb again. The small jar where she kept the special herbs was empty; she had used them all.

She needed to look for Kunutum, her best friend in the *gagû*, a *nadītu* a little older then she was who was an authority on herbs and medicines. Amat-Šamaš wanted Kunutum's companionship even more than the herbs.

"Amat-Šamaš, you look terrible," her old friend asked with concern. "What happened? The headaches again?"

"Yes, but it's more than that. Iltani will be arriving next week in time for the festival of Šamaš." She paused, gazing away. "I should be happy, I know, but there is something that pains me a great deal, something I have not told anyone before. It is something from my past."

"My dear friend, I see your great distress, your wrinkled brow, the way you press your head between your palms. Let me give you a potion," she said, and went to pound a mixture of herbs in a small pot and brew it with water on the coals. A healing, aromatic smell filled the air.

"Here, drink this," Kunutum said, handing her a cup of the remedy, and waited patiently for her friend to unburden herself.

Amat-Šamaš sipped slowly and felt her body unwind. The time had come, she knew. She could trust Kunutum to keep her secret. But how to tell the story?

Closing her eyes, she started at the beginning, while Kunutun sat there listening in disbelief to the painful memories of her friend.

After a while, Amat-Šamaš stopped talking. Her gaze was absent, as if she was somewhere else. Kunutum had a hundred questions. But she held her tongue; she was there to listen, nothing else.

Haggard though she was now, Amat-Šamaš felt comforted.

"Thank you for listening, dear Kunutum," she said. "Now you understand why Iltani's presence will be painful for me. I am afraid the memories will haunt me again."

Amat-Šamaš stayed for the evening meal with Kunutum. She was not sure what had brought on the relief, the potion or talking about the past or Kunutum's company. By the time she went home, she felt much better; she even dared to hope that having Iltani with her now would somehow make up for her own lost childhood and heal the anguish of the past.

Chapter 5

TEMPLE MUSICIANS PLAYED THEIR DRUMS in a steady beat as they accompanied the priests coming for Iltani. As the procession approached Iltani's house, the sounds of the drumming intensified. Any moment, the family would leave for the temple. The gifts, the food, the dresses, everything she would take to the *gagû*, was packed and ready. There was a great bustle in the courtyard and Iltani took shelter in *Abu's* library.

Her heart raced as the drums approached, louder, faster, louder, faster.

They were in luck, though, the weather was good for the month of Tebêtu, which was usually wet and cold. Today the sky was clear. Iltani wore her indigo dress and fine new leather sandals lined with lamb's wool against the cold. For the procession to the *gagû*, Iltani decided to wear the beautiful shawl Šamhat had presented to her at the feast.

"Iltani," she heard *Ummu* call, "do you hear the drums? It's time to go. The priest and the servants will be here soon."

Ummu and *Abu* waited in the courtyard. Iltani walked outside, rubbing her eyes. Sin-rēmēni threw himself on her with all his might. "I'll miss you so much," he said and buried his face in her dress.

Iltani could hardly breathe. She knew that for the first two years, she would not be allowed to leave the premises of the *gagû*, except to go to the temple or in case of a death in the family. She had never been separated from Sin-rēmēni for more than a day or two. The pain of separation was unbearable now, but she was determined not to let her feelings show. If she needed to cry, she would cry later, when no one was around.

"Come, my girl," she heard *Ummu* call.

A resinous smell of pine torches filled the air. The procession had arrived. Two priests accompanied by servants filed into the courtyard.

"May *Šamaš* bless this house! May he grant you good health forever," the priest said, blessing *Ummu* and *Abu*.

"May *Šamaš* grant you good health." *Abu* returned the blessing.

"My servants will carry the hampers to the temple," said the priest, beckoning the servants. The servants bound the hampers to their backs with leather straps and stood up in unison, as though obeying a silent signal.

Abu and *Ummu* looked on, both silent, *Ummu* with concern for Iltani's welfare, *Abu* with sadness. Of all his children, he felt closest to Iltani. She was his comfort. Nevertheless, he was also gratified that she had come this far and brought so much honor to the family. He knew she would be happy and well occupied in the *gagû*. Two years of separation was not so long a time.

* * *

"Bride of Šamaš, I lead you now to the temple for your offering and feast," the priest intoned in a loud, clear voice. They wended their way through the streets of Sippar, shiny beads of torch light quivering to the beat of drums. Onlookers bowed as they passed, praising the gods.

Iltani walked behind *Abu* and *Ummu*, with Sin-rēmēni close by. Šamhat and the other members of the family awaited them at the temple. Iltani watched the scene unfolding in a daze. She had a fluttery feeling in her stomach; this was her final farewell.

By the time they reached the temple gates, the sky had turned a fiery red.

The procession wound into a large vestibule at the foot of the Ziggurat, used only for special occasions, like this annual three-day festival when the new *nadītu* entered the *gagû*.

Iltani could see her siblings Marduk-ili and Šamhat with the other families sitting around small trays of fresh fruit and dates, bread and jugs of beer. They were enjoying themselves, talking animatedly.

The entrance on the other side of the vestibule led to a courtyard just below the Ziggurat steps. Iltani saw smoke rise to the darkening sky. Her offering to Šamaš was on its way. Lyres, flutes, and drums played softly somewhere and Iltani observed the scene in quiet wonder. She was about to follow *Ummu* and *Abu* as they headed with Sin-rēmēni toward Marduk-ili and Šamhat and the rest of the family, when she felt a firm hand on her shoulder.

"Come, my dear," said an unknown woman, directing her away from them into the inner courtyard where the altar stood. Iltani saw traces of blood on the floor and she tried to avert her eyes from the sight of the sacrificed animal. Her gaze fell on the massive steps of the sacred Ziggurat. She had seen it many times before, but only from afar. And now, here she stood, at the foot of the stairs to the dwelling-place of the gods.

"Come, it is time for the *nadītu* to enter the *gagû*. We must get you ready."

"What do you mean?" Iltani asked in surprise.

"You will see," said the woman with a smile. "And call me Reš-Aja."

Reš-Aja led Iltani into a heated room with a strong smell of incense. Six *nadītu* standing along the wall smiled in greeting, each one holding a small colorful vessel.

Iltani felt intimidated by the group of strange women. Reš-Aja pulled a long, heavy drape across the entrance, and approached her in a whisper: "Now you will be anointed into the *gagû* and your new sisterhood, as befitting a bride of

Šamaš and Aja. When you leave this room, you will bring your offering to the gods, and there will be an exchange of bridal gifts, and after that you will be fully one of us."

An ancient looking *nadītu* with a knot of long white hair moved toward Iltani with a cup in one hand and a large cloth in the other.

"Here, child, drink this slowly, carefully. You may find it to be somewhat strong for your taste."

Iltani took the cup from her hand and smelled the syrupy liquid.

She took a sip that burned her throat, but then a warm, fuzzy sweetness pervaded her. She had never tasted anything like this. Slowly, she emptied the cup and gave it back to the *nadītu*.

Something seemed different now. The room was hotter than before, with thick clouds of incense: intoxicating, bitter and sweet. Her body felt lighter; she hovered in the air. Four *nadītu* women began to undress Iltani, leaving her in her undershirt. Normally, she would have felt ashamed to stand like this in front of strangers, but the drink had put her in a trance, carefree.

The *nadītu* drew close and Iltani felt their hands stroking her lightly all over with perfumed oil as they hummed a strange tune. The incense blending with the perfumed oil made her shut her eyes and bask in the sensations, letting go of every thought. Soon she was dressed in her own clothes again. When she opened her eyes, she saw Reš-Aja standing before her with a basket of barley and myrrh.

"Iltani," she said, handing her the basket, "this will be your first offering to Šamaš and Aja, with barley for their food and myrrh for their incense."

On the altar outside, Iltani placed her offering to the gods, and a powerful aroma wafted through the air.

When Iltani entered the vestibule again, the chief priest signaled the musicians to stop playing: "Brothers and sisters," he announced, "now begins the celebration of *sebut šattim*, the festival for our god Šamaš here in Sippar. We have sacrificed three sheep and a goat in devotion to Šamaš. The new *nadītu* have offered Šamaš and Aja barley and myrrh. Approach new *nadītu*, for the ceremony of the rope."

Iltani and the other new *nadītu* approached the priest. One was a little older, the second about Iltani's age. Iltani smiled at them, trying to be friendly. The older girl nodded and smiled in appreciation; the stern-faced younger girl did not return her smile, but continued to glower at her family.

At a signal from the priest, a servant presented him with three extraordinary ropes made of twined cotton and decorated with carnelian beads and small shiny golden round plaques.

The priest took one rope, drew close to the older *nadītu* and tied it around her wrist. "This will bind you to Šamaš, the god of justice, and his consort, Aja. Stay faithful to them, and they will guide you always and protect you from evil demons and malevolent spirits and predators who wish you harm."

Then the priest tied ropes around each *nadītu's* wrist. When he had completed the ceremony, there was more music and chanting, and then another priest came forward and addressed the *nadītu*:

"May Šamaš and Aja keep you forever healthy. Today the *gagû* welcomes you. From this day forward you belong to Šamaš and Aja. They will be your *Abu* and *Ummu*, they will preserve you and bestow their love and abundance on you. To them you will bring the *piqqitu*, your daily offering. Tomorrow we celebrate the festival of Šamaš, and the following day will be devoted to the memory of those who have departed to their faiths. May Marduk, Šamaš and Aja bless you and forever keep you healthy."

At this, servants entered bearing trays of meat and fish, fresh bread, and vegetables.

Iltani sat next to *Abu*, hardly tasting the food, scarcely conscious of the gifts presented to each *nadītu*: a lyre, superbly carved, and cotton-stuff, finely woven and dyed, a rare and precious cloth.

The musicians played on and the temple-slaves performed a lively dance.

As the feast drew to a close, there was some crying and commotion.

Iltani kissed her parents goodbye. Sin-rēmēni had fallen asleep in the servant's arms. Iltani kissed his cheeks and when he clung to her in a dream, she burst out crying, unable to hold back any longer. Marduk-ili and Šamhat embraced her and blessed her by the gods.

Abu hugged her for a long time and whispered, "I will miss you very much, my little girl." And with that he left, hiding his own tears. *Ummu* too wept, as she kissed Iltani over and over. "I will miss you very much. I love you, my sweet daughter. May the gods protect you."

So tired she could barely stand, Iltani watched them walk away. And now she was alone. Amat-Šamaš beckoned a *nadītu* to help her lead Iltani home.

* * *

Two more days of festivities followed in the *gagû* for temple priests and priestesses, votaries, and *nadītu*. Iltani felt like an observer, far from home. She felt strange and helpless with only her aunt to talk to, a person she hardly knew. She could not find Tabbija anywhere. That made the situation even harder. She had needed so urgently to see her friend again.

The servant woke her before dawn, so she could be the first to bring offerings to the temple, as expected of a new initiate during the first three days. By evening, she was exhausted. As soon as she lay on her bed, she fell asleep.

The final day of the festivities passed quickly enough and Iltani felt almost cheerful returning to her new quarters, but again, she was so tired, she fell asleep in her clothes.

Chapter 6

IT TOOK ILTANI A MOMENT TO REALIZE where she was: the unfamiliar room at aunt Amat-Šamaš's house in the *gagû*. Though she had slept there for the last two nights of the festivities, it was nearly dark when she returned, and she had left the house so early in the morning. There had been no time to look around and reflect.

The room was pleasing. The walls were sand-colored, but the coarse woolen carpet and bright cushions contrasted nicely. Propped against the facing wall was the gift from *Ummu* and *Abu*, the wooden chest, inlaid with miniature ivory carvings and ornamented with cornelian beads.

Iltani walked over to the chest. Although *Abu* had shown it to her briefly at home during her feast, only now did she see how exquisite it was. She ran her fingers over the lid, following the contours of the ivory miniatures. When she opened it, she found nothing inside but a tightly woven reed mat that protected the wood from the damp.

A voice startled Iltani. "Good morning." Mattaki, Amat-Šamaš's servant, peeked out at her from behind the curtain. "It is mid-day already and I thought perhaps I should wake you up. I have prepared some dough and dried fruit for you. Would you like to get dressed and come out to the courtyard?"

"Thank you, I will," Iltani replied, though she was uncertain where her clothes were. Looking around, she spotted a simple reed hamper. Inside, she remembered, were her dresses and the other clothes she had brought from home. She chose the cream-colored dress and smoothed it out on her mattress. Before dressing, she washed her face and drank some cool water from the jug in the corner.

* * *

"You've already had a visitor," said Mattaki as Iltani sat down to wait for her pita bread to bake.

"A young *nadītu* came by early this morning before setting off for the temple, but I did not want to disturb your sleep. Her name is Tabbija. She said she would come by again later today."

"And where is my aunt Amat-Šamaš?" Iltani asked.

"She went to the temple. She said she would be home much later. If you like, I'll take you around the *gagû* and show you some of the important places here," Mattaki offered.

"That would be extremely kind."

After the light repast, they set out to explore the *gagû* together.

Mattaki showed Iltani some of the grander houses, especially the one belonging to Hammurabi's sister, the Princess, decorated with inscriptions on fired bricks and brilliant blue tiles.

"You know, some of the wealthier *nadītu* have beautiful houses too, but they don't compare with this one, a tribute from King Hammurabi to his sister," Mattaki said.

"The tiles are glorious, and look at the script. It's Sumerian," Iltani said.

"When the building was completed, there was a great feast. The King himself presided."

"Now here's a most important place," Mattaki said.

Iltani regarded the building. It was of average size, not decorated in any special way from the outside, except for the burned clay-bricks, used mostly in imperial buildings, like temples and palaces.

"What is this?" Iltani asked.

"It's the bathhouse. The High Priest of the temple makes sure it is kept clean and well-run."

"I have never been to a bathhouse before." Iltani said, curious.

"Since it is unseemly for a *nadītu* to bathe in the river, water is diverted from the canals into the bathhouse and heated there in winter so that the *nadītu* may immerse themselves in privacy and comfort. It was the wish of the Princess to build a bathhouse here, from the kindness of her heart," Mattaki explained.

They passed the bathhouse and the quarters of various *gagû* officials and their servants.

Iltani tried to memorize the layout of the lanes so she could find her way around by herself next time.

"This house belongs to Kunutum. She is a close friend of your aunt's and she has a special knowledge of herbs. There is a *gagû* physician, too, but he lives elsewhere, outside the compound, so when a *nadītu* needs help, she usually comes to Kunutum."

They walked towards the gate which connected the *gagû* directly to the Šamaš temple and peeked through at the crowd that was talking loudly in the courtyard. Iltani surveyed the enormous courtyard, for the first time from this viewpoint, through this gate. She felt a jolt of excitement.

A man sitting on a high chair silenced them.

"Is that a trial in progress?" Iltani asked.

"It must be. I often see the same man presiding as judge. Look they brought out the emblem of the god. It looks as though they're about to swear an oath, and then the trial will be over."

Iltani observed the scene with interest. She paid special attention to the scribe writing on a clay tablet.

"Do the *nadītu* ever take part in trials?" Iltani wondered.

"Why yes, many do. The family of the deceased *nadītu* who adopted your aunt Amat-Šamaš sued her once over the property she inherited, including the house you live in. Amat-Šamaš was able to prove to the judge she was in the right and so she won the case."

There was still much to see but Mattaki had to finish preparing dinner, so they walked along the small canal that ran through the *gagû*. A tall and rather stout *nadītu* walked by and stopped to greet them.

"You must be Amat-Šamaš's niece. What a lovely girl you are. Welcome to the *gagû*," she said, eyeing Iltani.

"I will tell Amat-Šamaš you said hello, Mistress Bēltani," said Mattaki respectfully, yet pulling Iltani away.

Iltani looked back. The *nadītu* was a little daunting.

"Who is that?" she asked Mattaki.

"Bēltani is one of the more influential members of the *gagû*, and quite wealthy. She is the daughter of a prominent priest of the Marduk temple in Babylon."

No sooner had they reached home, than Tabbija dashed into the courtyard and embraced Iltani with a little shout of joy.

"Iltani, my friend, you're here at last!" she exclaimed. "I have so much to tell you." They hurried to Iltani's room and reclined on the cushions. Iltani was overjoyed to see her dear friend.

"So what is your impression of the *gagû*? Do you know anyone here besides your aunt Amat-Šamaš and me? And how was your initiation?" Tabbija asked.

"Well, I, it is all so new. I am . . . by the gods! What happened to you?" Iltani howled out loud as she took a good look at Tabbija and was stunned by her friend's voluptuous figure. "If I recall, the last time I saw you, your figure was more like mine?" She noted in wonder. Iltani was fairly thin, her breasts rather small and undeveloped.

"I left when I was sixteen, you forget. I guess I've grown up over the past few years," Tabbija answered her with a confident smile.

But Iltani noticed that her eyes were not so happy. Tabbija was still the irrepressible girl she remembered, yet there was something different about her now, besides her changed body, a certain gloominess coming from her depths. It was hard to tell. Things change, after all, and they had not seen each other for over three years.

"So tell me, do you like the *gagû*, Iltani," Tabbija asked.

Iltani did not know where to begin. "I think it will take me a few days to understand the changes in my life," she said. "All I thought about before I came to the *gagû* was my training to be a real scribe. But when I said goodbye to *Ummu* and *Abu*, I realized that I would be separated from my family and my home and everything I knew."

"Well you are fortunate that your aunt has adopted you and that you have a home with her here. I rent a room in the house of another *nadītu*. But I like the arrangement; this way I do not feel alone."

Tabbija noticed the beautiful wooden chest.

"That was a parting gift from *Abu* and *Ummu*," Iltani said.

"Leaving those you love behind is hard," said Tabbija.

Iltani clearly saw the desolation in her eyes. What was wrong? she wondered. "Tabbija, I kept looking for you at the *gagû* festival. Where were you?" she asked, and suddenly discerned that her friend was holding her forehead as if in pain." What is it Tabbija? Is it your health?" asked Iltani, taking her hand.

"I am in good health, thanks to Šamaš and Aja. I am fine, I am fine, just my head," Tabbija replied, letting go of Iltani's hand and sinking back into the cushion. "So, this is the future you always dreamed of. When do you start your lessons? And with whom?"

"I will study with Amat-Mamu, for now the only female scribe in the *gagû*. She is supposed to be very good, they say."

Tabbija was about to speak again when they heard Mattaki greet Amat-Šamaš in the courtyard.

"I will go now," said Tabbija, jumping up from the cushion. She embraced Iltani. "I am so happy you are here. I will come to visit you again soon," she said, and left, greeting Amat-Šamaš on her way out.

"Iltani," she heard her aunt call her. "Come join us in the courtyard."

With a pale smile, Amat-Šamaš listened to Iltani's account of her tour with Mattaki. But she had to leave again, an errand, she said, so Iltani and Mattaki would have to eat without her.

Iltani helped Mattaki prepare dinner and ate without much appetite. She retreated to her room, washed herself and curled up on the mattress. Why was her aunt so cool and distant? Or was she imagining things? She felt alone, homesick for *Abu* and *Ummu* and Sin-rēmēni, and even to Shima-ahati, the servant. "You are not a baby," she chided herself. She fell asleep quickly.

* * *

Next morning Amat-Šamaš accompanied Iltani to the Šamaš temple for the daily offering. They entered by the *gagû* gate.

Iltani's body trembled from excitement, her heart beating faster. It was the first time she entered the temple as a *nadītu*. Would anyone know the difference? she wondered. It was the hour of worship reserved for *nadītu*, as most of them preferred not to offer with the common mass. Iltani was tremulous as she offered the barley and dried figs, and entreated the gods to guide her way. A few other *nadītu* greeted her aunt, and smiled at her. Iltani was happy to join their circle.

The visit to the temple and the walk back went by so fast, Iltani wondered what to do the rest of the day. Her aunt went off somewhere, declining Iltani's request to join her. At home, she would be helping *Ummu* at this hour, or playing with Sin-rēmēni or watching *Abu* work in the library. Perhaps she would pay a visit to Tabbija. Mattaki might know where she lived. She walked to the cooking room and looked around. It was similar to the one at home, with shelves of jars and piles of baskets and reed hampers of various sizes filled with vegetables.

Mattaki, sitting on a mat, looked up at her.

"Can I get you something?"

"Well actually," Iltani said hesitantly, "I thought I might help you prepare the dinner. I have nothing to do until my lessons begin."

"All right. There's only a little barley left in the jar. Could you husk some more for me? You'll find a bunch of stalks in the big chest outside."

Iltani was happy to comply and brought the stalks back to the cooking room. This would be a good opportunity to get to know Mattaki better and find out more about the *gagû*.

"How did you come to work in the *gagû*?" Iltani asked.

"My husband was a master carpenter many years ago. He had an accident, a heavy log crushed his hand one day, and since then, my eldest son has been running the business. But he was not as talented as his father, and we earned less, so I hired myself out as a servant. The first *nadītu* I worked for was a neighbor of the one who adopted Amat-Šamaš, so I became acquainted with Amat-Šamaš just before she herself became a *nadītu*. By the time she had the means to hire a servant, she hired me and I have been with her ever since. But I am so old now I should stop working soon."

Iltani knew very little of her aunt's history, so she asked Mattaki and was surprised by her reluctance to talk about it. All she would say was that Amat-Šamaš herself would tell

Iltani when the time was right. Why was her aunt so secretive? Why did she avoid Iltani?

"Iltani, are you here?" it was Tabbija's voice. She sounded happy, animated.

Iltani looked questioningly at Mattaki. "Yes, go. Meet your friend, enjoy yourself."

* * *

"I want to take you to my house, so you'll know where I live. And then I want to hear all about the past years." Tabbija took Iltani's hand and led her across the *gagû*.

"This is nice," Iltani said as she looked around the room. It was bigger than Iltani's own room, admirably furnished with a table, chairs and a sitting niche with bright cushions. A thick woolen carpet made the room warm and welcoming, and two ample reed chests lined the wall. Phials of oil in various sizes lay scattered everywhere and piled on the mattress was a colorful jumble of clothes, a cheerful mess.

"Come let's sit here," Tabbija said, inviting Iltani next to her on the cushion.

"I still cannot believe we are here together. Doesn't it seem like yesterday that we whispered all night together on the roof? And remember the time we were playing hide and seek and I got stuck in the big hamper in your pantry?" Tabbija recalled.

"Yes, and when we finally pulled you out, your hair was full of dough," Iltani said, laughing.

"Those were easy days, full of play and frolic," said Tabbija, and her eyes welled up with gloom.

"Are you all right? You seem sad. Are your *Ummu* and *Abu* in good health?" Iltani asked.

Tabbija began to pace around the room. She stopped and looked at Iltani for a moment, then covered her face and moaned. "Oh, Iltani, I don't want to tell you, not until you've settled in here. But I do not want to conceal the truth from you."

"We used to share everything," Iltani encouraged her.

"This is not about pinching the good cakes from the kitchen."

"Yes, I understand." Iltani answered gravely. "But I am still the same person, and I will keep your secret, whatever it may be."

"All right. You know, I never wished to become a *nadītu*, but my family left me no choice, and now. . ." she stopped, staring blankly in the air, "now I. . ." she searched for the word. "When my parents told me that this was their wish, I thought of the honor it would bring to the family, but I also grieved —no family, no husband, no children of my own. But I was an obedient daughter, sixteen years old, and I knew my parents wanted what was best for me. And then, over the past few months, everything changed, and I can no longer accept my life here, this life. . ."

Iltani waited quietly for her friend to continue.

"Do you remember Liwira-ana-ilim, the son of our servant? Since I entered the *gagû* he has been in charge of my lands. In my first two years here, the gatekeeper would deliver packages from him. But after that, I began to meet Liwira-ana-ilim myself. He brings me barley from the fields, barters with it and cares for all my needs. And then. . ." she looked straight at Iltani, "I began to feel something for Liwira-ana-ilim that I have never felt before. I wanted and needed to see him all the time. I missed him when he went home, and waited impatiently for the next time I needed something done and could call on him. Then a few months ago, when he brought my monthly supply of oil and barley, he gave me this. . ." She showed Iltani the small carnelian bead on a string that hung from her neck.

"He confessed his love, and at first I was stunned, frightened even. But I was also happier than I have ever been before. I realized I love him, too, very much. I want to be with him, not imprisoned here for the sake of family pride."

"Do your parents know, does anybody else know? What will happen if anyone finds out? You are a *nadītu*; you are obliged by law. Do you really think all the trouble you might cause for yourself and your family is worth it? Are you so miserable here?" Iltani asked in bewilderment.

Tabbija felt that perhaps she had been wrong to confide in Iltani. They understood life so differently now. Iltani was still an innocent maiden, while she herself had turned into a passionate woman. She would wither and die in the *gagû*.

"No, this life is not enough for me. I want more: a family, a husband, children. Please try to understand. You are the only one who knows about this Iltani, and I trust you not to tell anyone."

"I won't, I promise," Iltani said quietly.

"Come, I'll walk you home. It's getting late," Tabbija said. Saying those words aloud, Tabbija felt, had been a first step on her newly chosen path. She would leave the *gagû*, even if it meant relinquishing all her worldly possessions. A life with the man she loved, the man who loved her, was all she wanted.

* * *

That night Iltani lay in her bed, thinking about the *gagû*. As long as she could remember she wanted to be there, her father groomed her for this position. She had never considered the possibility that other women in the *gagû* felt otherwise.

Were there other *nadītu* like Tabbija who preferred to live outside the *gagû*? She recalled the night of the initiation, the scowling face of the young *nadītu*. Tabbija's story troubled her, deflated her. Something had changed. Her excitement about the *gagû* was tainted.

She had almost fallen asleep when she heard Amat-Šamaš in the courtyard. Iltani was certain that her aunt was avoiding her. Had it all been a mistake? Should she have fought her *Abu*, defied his wishes, and her own as well, married and had children instead of the life of a scribe?

No, she told herself. I have always wanted this path, to become a female scribe. The *gagû* was her only option. All beginnings are difficult, and I will work hard to fulfill my dream. Thinking these words made her feel a stronger.

Iltani was sound asleep when her aunt came into the room. Her aunt covered her gently and kissed her on the forehead.

"Talk to her, you must," said Mattaki later. "She is so young, and she misses her family."

"I know," said Amat-Šamaš with a loud sigh. "I know."

Chapter 7

ILTANI HAD NOT SEEN TABBIJA for two days, a long time to
contemplate the situation. Tabbija had made a choice, and
Iltani decided, as her friend, she was duty-bound to support
her. When they met again, Iltani revealed her concerns, and
so did Tabbija.

Tabbija spoke very little about Liwira-ana-ilim except
to say that he was extremely able and hardworking. In
addition to overseeing Tabbija's land, he managed the
property of an elderly couple who were childless and well
off. He hoped that in return they would adopt him and
leave their land to him when they died.

During the three days festivities, when she knew no
one would miss her, she had escaped from the *gagû* to meet
Liwira-ana-ilim. Her face was radiant as she confessed. Iltani
did not ask, but assumed there was no real physical
relationship between Tabbija and Liwira-ana-ilim, otherwise
she might have conceived a child, and if she had, that the
gagû authorities would probably take serious measures
against her.

Iltani did not know that Tabbija, the daughter of a
physician, had been refining her natural skills she had
inherited form her father, and used herbs as a means of
contraception.

"I'm lonely. I have never been alone before, without
my family. It is so difficult," Iltani said.

"You have your aunt here. She's family, isn't she?"

"Yes, but I don't know. She avoids me."

"How so?"

"She never takes me anywhere, she rarely eats with me, she hardly speaks, and when she does, she keeps the conversations short."

"Perhaps she's unaccustomed to having people around. She's lived so many years on her own. The *nadītu* I live with more or less ignored me at first, but in time, she got used to me, and today we are friends. But I did not tell her about Liwira-ana-ilim."

"Maybe you're right about Amat-Šamaš. But I have the feeling there's more to it than that." Iltani hugged her knees, curling up. "Most of all I miss Sin-rēmēni," Iltani whispered.

"Give it time," Tabbija said, putting her arm around her. "You'll feel better once you start your lessons with the scribe. Many of the *nadītu* don't want to be here at first, but eventually they find peace, and so will you. I am not the typical *nadītu*. You would not believe how clever and accomplished some *nadītu* are. A few of them have tripled their inheritance, living a very luxurious life."

"I suppose you're right. I shouldn't feel sorry for myself. I am, after all, where I want to be," Iltani answered.

* * *

"Have something to eat. You will be hungry later on," said Mattaki to Iltani.

"I can't. I feel a fluttering in my stomach. Amat-Mamu's servant will be here any moment." She ran to see if anyone was at the entrance.

She had finally received an invitation from Amat-Mamu to come for her first lesson in the scribal arts, and the servant would be coming to take her to Amat-Mamu's house.

"At least eat some dried figs, they are so sweet," said Mattaki. Iltani took one from the bowl, her hands trembling with excitement. She almost knocked over a jug of beer. What a bad omen that would have been, she thought with relief.

A plumpish woman entered the courtyard. "May Aja protect this house and those who live in it," she said in a high pitched voice. "You must be Iltani. I have come to take you to Amat-Mamu. Are you ready?"

"Yes, yes." Iltani jumped up and smoothed her dress to make a good impression.

* * *

Amat-Mamu's house looked enormous. From the courtyard, Iltani counted five entrances to the different rooms, more than her own family had. The servant led her to a room full of tablets that were scattered on wooden shelves along the wall and packed into reed hampers on the floor. Everywhere she looked, she saw clay tablets in different sizes.

"By Šamaš and Aja!" she exclaimed in astonishment. There were far more clay tablets here then her father had. She had never seen so many in one room before.

"Please do not touch anything until Amat-Mamu arrives," said the servant, and with a nod of her head, she left the room.

Iltani had to fight the urge to pick up one of the tablets. But she would never have done such a thing without permission. There were several cushions on the floor and beside them a small basket and a pile of styluses and unshaped reeds. Iltani tried to imagine what they would do this first lesson. Perhaps Amat-Mamu will be interested in what she has learned with *Abu*, or ask her to inscribe a few signs. That's what she hoped at least. Whatever happened, she told herself, she would do her best and not take offense if Amat-Mamu treated her harshly, as *Abu* had warned she might.

"Ah, you're here," said Amat-Mamu hurriedly as she walked in. Amat-Mamu was shorter by a half a head than Iltani. She was a compact, plump little woman, with grey hair secured tightly in a knot.

"Your first lesson will consist of watching me write an urgent letter," she said taking clay out of the hamper and a few reed styluses. "Don't just stand there," she said beckoning Iltani, who was too perplexed to move. "And whatever you see, you must not, I repeat, you must not say a word or make a noise, even if you're startled."

Iltani followed Amat-Mamu out of the house, fearful and disappointed. Where was her teacher taking her? She was walking so fast Iltani could hardly keep up. So they would not read or write anything today, it seemed.

Amat-Mamu did not slow down or talk as they crossed the *gagû*. None of the houses looked familiar and Iltani was sure, that left alone here, she would have been terribly lost. They stopped at a small house. "Not a word," Amat-Mamu put her finger to her lips as they entered the courtyard. The house was even smaller than her aunt's, and badly in need of repair. In the courtyard stood an older *nadītu*, holding a clay pot over burning coal. "She is inside; she awaits you. I have given her a soothing remedy to drink, but the bruises and wounds . . . are very bad. She will need time and my best herbs to heal."

Iltani was frightened. What had happened? Apparently something very bad. But who would dare hurt a *nadītu*? They . . . we, she reminded herself, are under the protection of Šamaš and Aja. Anyone who tries to hurt us will incur the wrath of the gods.

As they entered a small room, Iltani, following close behind, saw a woman sitting on a mattress. The woman's eyes were red and swollen from crying. But what was worse, there were raw lash marks on her arms and legs. It looked as though she had been severely whipped. She was dressed in a thin white shift that revealed the bleeding gashes on her back. Iltani was so distressed by the sight she wanted to run away.

"Tell me what happened," Amat-Mamu said soothingly, no longer brusque.

Eli-eresa, the young *nadītu*, spoke slowly.

"I sewed a garment for a man named Sin-iddinam and delivered it to him. He promised he would pay me the following day, but when I went to collect what he owed me, he did not pay. A day passed, a week passed, still he did not pay. I sent three messengers and they all came back empty-handed. When three months had gone by, I went to see him again, but he would only agree to pay me half the sum. When I went to see him again, instead of paying me what he still owed me, he gave me a thrashing."

The room was so quiet Iltani was afraid they could hear her breathing.

"And what is worse," Eli-eresa continued, "he bragged that he beat five other *nadītu*. How could such a thing happen? How did we not know of this?" she asked in anguish. "Why did those *nadītu* not report it to the overseer, Rapaš-ṣilli-Ea?"

Iltani was so shaken she barely noticed that Amat-Mamu had had been taking down Eli-eresa's story on a clay tablet.

"Here, I have written a letter," said Amat-Mamu. "Not to the overseer but to a judge. I'll deliver it to him myself if you like. Shall I read it to you?"

Eli-eresa nodded.

"To my lord say; thus (says) Eli-eresa.

I sold Sin-iddinam son of Ilšu-bani, a citizen of my city, Sippar, a garment. After he wore the garment for three months, he paid me a lower price, holding back half a shekel from the original price of the garment.

I went to him, to remind him to give me the rest of the money, but instead he beat me viciously; as if I were not a servant of Šamaš.

He has treated me in a way which is not acceptable in this land!

The next day I went to him, and said: "Why have you treated me this way?"

Thus he said: "I have beaten five nadītu of Šamaš, besides you.

I will pay only those I wish to pay! No one takes anything from me."

My lord, you are my judge, pass a verdict on the case I have with Sin-iddinam."

As they were leaving, Iltani noticed the older *nadītu* was smearing a brown ointment on Eli-eresa's wounds. This woman looked familiar, yet Iltani could not remember from where.

Amat-Mamu was silent all the way back and Iltani was too distraught to ask any questions.

Just before reaching the house, Amat-Mamu turned to Iltani and asked: "What did you learn today that is worth remembering?"

Iltani was speechless. What had she learned today that was worth remembering? Nothing about the art of the scribe. What she had learned was that all her notions about the life of a *nadītu* were perhaps the notions of a silly child, provided to her by her trusting *Abu*. That was her lesson for today.

Amat-Mamu observed her, waiting for a response. As none came, she said: "A scribe should be seen and not heard. And our services are not limited to those who pay us to write down and witness their business contracts. As *nadītu* scribes we must help our friends. I know that you will never forget what you saw today and that will make you a better scribe. A scribe whose hand competes with his mouth is indeed a scribe. A scribe who writes without error and without asking the speaker to repeat himself need never sew garments for a living." Amat-Mamu held Iltani's gaze until Iltani looked down at her feet and said, "Yes, Mistress, I understand."

* * *

When Iltani arrived at home she found her aunt Amat-Šamaš sitting in the garden.

"How was your first lesson?" she asked.

Iltani ran to her room and fell on her mattress, her body shaking with sobs.

Amat-Šamaš, who had kept her distance until now, could not but feel for the girl. Beginnings were hard on every *nadītu*, even those as cheerful and lively as Iltani. She entered Iltani's room, sat down next to her and stroked her hair.

"What is it Iltani?" she asked softly, removing some of the mental boundaries she had set.

Lying face down in her despair, Iltani told her aunt what had happened. Amat-Šamaš stroked her hair, the first sign of affection she had ever shown. Soothed and comforted, Iltani's sobbing subsided.

Amat-Šamaš was torn. She longed to be close to Iltani, to offer her the warmth and protection she needed, yet she dreaded the consequences of revealing her secret. How would it affect Iltani, Iltani's mother, the honor of the family? Seeing this young girl, facing hardship so courageously, she let down her guard—for both their sakes. After all, one day she would need Iltani to nurse her, perhaps even sooner than she imagined.

"Come, Iltani, let's have something to drink in the garden. That will make you feel better," and she stood up, waiting for Iltani to follow.

Iltani, picked herself up from the mattress, washed her face and joined Amat-Šamaš. They spoke about the days ahead, and Amat-Šamaš told Iltani about her friend Kunutum, but not about the past which had brought her to the *gagû*. Tentatively, cautiously, she allowed Iltani into her heart.

The following morning Iltani accompanied Amat-Šamaš to the temple, yet when she asked to join her at other times, her aunt declined.

* * *

A few days later, Amat-Mamu's servant came again to fetch Iltani for her second lesson. This time Iltani was more apprehensive about going. However once in Amat-Mamu's room, after being reminded not to touch anything, she gazed around in amazement. Again she was mesmerized by the quantity of tablets in the room. The smell of clay reminded her of her father's library.

"May Šamaš and Aja keep you well," said Amat-Mamu as she entered. Iltani greeted her and awaited her instructions.

"How is your Sumerian?" asked Amat-Mamu.

"Not very good. I know a few words, a smattering of signs."

"Well, that is the first thing you will have to learn. A scribe worthy of the name must know how to read and write Sumerian."[1]

Amat-Mamu examined the tablets on the shelf, picked one up and handed it to Iltani. Then she took clay and two reed styluses from the hamper and set them down on the mat beside Iltani.

"Let's begin with this," she said, having deftly shaped the clay into a tablet small enough to fit into her palm and engraved a sign. "This is DINGIR. It can mean Anum, the sky god, or merely sky or god. Or when used in Akkadian, it merely stands for the sound *an*."

Iltani already knew that sign but decided not to boast, sensing that Amat-Mamu would not like it.

"This is the sign for É in Sumerian and *bītum* (house) in Akkadian. When you add GAL, meaning *rabûm* (great) in Akkadian you have É.GAL which means *ekallum* (the palace)."

Amat-Mamu taught Iltani five more Sumerian signs and explained their alternate functions in Akkadian. Iltani

---

[1] In the time of Iltani's life (the Old Babylonian period), Sumerian was not used as a spoken language anymore, but was considered imperative and was studied, just as Latin was in the Middle Ages.

concentrated as well as she could; it was not easy to remember everything.

Amat-Mamu showed Iltani how to press the signs into the damp clay and Iltani copied them one by one, repeating the functions Amat-Mamu had just taught her. That done, Amat-Mamu brought her a middle-sized tablet, divided vertically, with a sign on one side and several signs facing it.

"This is the list all scribes must learn by heart—the Sumerian signs are on the left and the Akkadian equivalents are on the right."

Some of the signs, Iltani saw, were the same she had just pressed into the practice-tablet.

"Take this tablet home with you and by next lesson learn all the Sumerian words, and their meanings, and all the other values in Akkadian. Practice inscribing them and when you're sure you've mastered them, make a good, clean copy of this tablet for yourself, and bring this one back to me. One of my servants will walk you home with more clay and reeds to work with. I assume you know how to sharpen your own reed stylus," she said rather than asked.

"Yes I do. Thank you for the lesson," Iltani answered. She wanted to tell Amat-Mamu how thrilled she was to begin the real curriculum, but feared she would not approve of such exuberance.

"I will send my servant to fetch you for your lesson next week. I am sure you will be quite busy until then." She stood up and summoned a servant to accompany Iltani home with a supply of clay and a bundle of reeds.

On the way back, Iltani reviewed the new signs in her mind. She was excited again. She felt alive. The difficult beginning was over now, it seemed. Her aunt was warming up to her, and she was finally learning the art of the scribe, just like a pupil in the É-DUBBA. She returned home with a new lightness of heart.

Chapter 8

WINTER IN THE *GAGÛ* WAS HARDER than at home. More
than ever Iltani missed Sin-rēmēni and the way they used to
snuggle together to keep warm and cozy.

She remembered the funny stories she used to tell him,
making them both laugh so hard *Ummu* would yell at them
to be quiet. Here she slept alone.

* * *

"Are you all right, Amat-Šamaš? Why are you leaning
your head on your hands? You look very pale," said Iltani
one cold evening as they sat together in Amat-Šamaš's
room.

"It will pass, Iltani, do not be alarmed. It's hard to
believe you've been here over two months already," she
said, quickly changing the subject. "This winter is colder
than last. I am looking forward to spring."

"Yes, me too," Iltani added.

"Tell me about your *Ummu*, what is she like?" Amat-
Šamaš asked.

Iltani was surprised by the question. Why would Amat-
Šamaš ask about her own sister? But then she remembered
what her mother had told her; her mother was born just as
Amat-Šamaš had left. So they did not grow up together.
How should she describe her?

"*Ummu* is good to us, though she is stricter and less
talkative than *Abu*. She works hard to run the household
and she seldom smiles, but when she does all her kindness
shows in her eyes, and that's what I love best about her.

And the fluffy bread she bakes for us," Iltani said with a laugh.

"Has she ever told you about her early girlhood?"

"No, not really, except to say that she grew up in a simple home in the south. But when I asked about *Ummu-ummu* and *Abu-ummu* all she told me was that they were good, humble folk, that they cared for her and loved her."

Iltani thought to ask Amat-Šamaš what these obscure people from the past were like. She was *Ummu's* older sister, after all. But something made her hold her tongue. "I suppose I was always closer to *Abu*," she added. "You know, since he is a scribe. I take after him, I think, and we have more to talk about."

"Do you think your *Ummu* has known happiness?" Amat-Šamaš asked.

"Well, yes. Sometimes I see her sitting next to *Abu* with her head on his shoulder while he talks or sings to us, and she smiles with contentment, the smile I love. Her marriage to *Abu* and her four children are her greatest blessings from the gods, she says. I used to hear my neighbors screaming all the time, but *Ummu* and *Abu* rarely quarrel. *Abu* loves her."

Amat-Šamaš continued to ask questions about the family all evening.

Iltani was relieved to see her aunt warming up and answered her with as much animation as she could muster. But she was worried about her aunt, who looked sallow, unwell. Iltani had become acquainted with Amat-Šamaš's friend Kunutum, the healer she had seen at her first scribal lesson tending the wounded *nadītu*. Kunutum gave Iltani remedies for Amat-Šamaš and showed her how to prepare them, and Iltani spent more and more time in her aunt's company. Sometimes she would sit with her quietly while she practiced her writing, and at other times they would talk.

Though Amat-Šamaš never requested her presence directly, Iltani could tell that she was pleased to be with her.

But Iltani was perplexed. Amat-Šamaš seemed to be fighting some inner war that concerned her. Then one cold winter day while she sat beside her aunt working on her Sumerian tablet, Amat-Šamaš began to reminisce about her early years in the *gagû*.

"My family was very poor and when I was about fifteen years old I had to earn a living so I sold myself into service. Little did I know that the woman who took me in was a vicious old *nadītu* who had frightened away many servants before me. I cleaned and cooked, I washed her clothing and bought food for her in the *kārum*. She worked me so hard I never had a moment's rest except for once in the summer when she allowed me to spend a day by the river. She used to cane me, too, so hard that one time Kunutum, who was a young *nadītu* then, took me away and treated my wounds with ointments made from herbs. Four years later, another *nadītu* came to my rescue."

"And who was she?" Iltani asked.

"She was a great-hearted *nadītu*. She took me on as a servant, and a year later, to my great fortune, she adopted me so that I became a *nadītu* even though my origins were humble. The *gagû* had no choice once she had made me her heir. And I continued to look after her until she died."

Amat-Šamaš told more and more stories about her early years in the *gagû*, but never about her previous life. Whenever Iltani asked she would merely change the subject. There must have been something painful about it she did not want to discuss.

Meanwhile Iltani worked diligently at her scribal lessons, practicing until her hands were covered with small cuts and blisters. The rest of the time she would meet with Tabbija, chatting about her lessons and reminiscing over their childhood mischiefs.

* * *

Amat-Mamu was certainly a rigorous teacher, as *Abu* had warned her. She would assign impossibly long lists of words for Iltani to memorize, more than required of scribal students at the É-DUBBA. Iltani missed the merriment with *Abu*, the stories and proverbs he used to introduce into her lessons. Amat-Mamu was strict and methodical. Iltani had to master an extended Sumerian vocabulary with all its grammatical convolutions, enough to make her eyes cross when added to the Akkadian equivalents and their diverse usages. However she was proud of the five tablets she had made on her own. Four contained lists of words, but the last tablet was a letter, a practice letter she had inscribed while her teacher was explaining a case. It was full of mistakes, of course, and missing signs, but Amat-Mamu had said, "Not bad for a first try." Iltani was happily surprised— Amat-Mamu had never said anything nice or encouraging to her before.

* * *

On one of the last mornings of Addaru, Iltani accompanied Amat-Mamu to the home of a wealthy *nadītu* who needed a letter.

"Bēltani is my best client. She commissions most of the letters and contracts I write. She is shrewd and successful in negotiation and has helped me secure my own fields and fortune. I am greatly in her debt. You must treat her with the utmost respect, think of her as a princess," said Amat-Mamu sternly.

She must indeed be important, thought Iltani, seeing that Amat-Mamu was not in the habit of discussing clients with her. This introduction made her feel vaguely nervous.

When they reached their destination and entered the main courtyard, Iltani was struck by the grandeur of the place. It was no bigger than Amat-Mamu's house, but the walls were decorated with elaborate bas-reliefs of animal figures in vivid shades of blue, green and red. The blue background showed up the flecks of gold and bright coloring of the lions and tigers and dragon-like creatures

71

that shimmered in the sunlight. Iltani had never seen anything like it.

"By Šamaš and Aja, this is magnificent," she exclaimed.

"Yes, indeed it is, not even the Princess has such beautiful decorations, though her house is splendid too. Come, let us go in."

Amat-Mamu led Iltani to a large room where Bēltani awaited them.

"There you are, very good. Let us begin," Bēltani said curtly with her eye on Iltani.

Iltani watched Amat-Mamu as Bēltani dictated the letters to her, yet she found it difficult to concentrate. Bēltani kept staring at Iltani with a look that unsettled her. When the session was over, Iltani was happy to go home.

* * *

That night she told Amat-Šamaš about the visit to Bēltani's house and the astonishing bas-relief. She did not mention the unpleasantness she had felt in Bēltani's presence. She supposed the fault was hers and not Bēltani's, since Bēltani had done nothing improper. In fact she had been very polite.

Later, as she was falling asleep, she heard Mattaki and her aunt whispering in the courtyard.

"But those are rumors, nothing more," said Amat-Šamaš.

"I hope you are right," Mattaki answered.

* * *

A few weeks later, Amat-Mamu presented Iltani with a new tablet to copy and learn at home, and gave her a curious task.

"You are to go to Bēltani's house and read for her. She requested you specifically."

"But what if I stumble over a sign or a word or even a whole sentence?" Iltani asked in dismay.

"Just try your best, Iltani. You have learned more than you know. I am sure you will do just fine," said her teacher.

"Take your time over each sign, read the whole word in your mind before you pronounce it out loud," she added.

One of Amat-Mamu's servants accompanied Iltani to show her the way.

Again she was dazzled by the splendor of the bas-reliefs on the walls and did not notice Bēltani standing right behind her.

"Magnificent, aren't they?" said Bēltani, startling Iltani. "I gaze at them many times a day as the sun travels across the sky. My favorite time is late morning when the flecks of gold begin to glitter like the sun on the canals."

"I have never seen anything so beautiful," Iltani said in awe.

"Come, Iltani. I would like you to read for me, a story you may know. I know this is your first time reading aloud to someone other than your teacher, but don't worry. You'll find me quite patient." Bēltani showed her into the room where they had sat the previous time.

Iltani tried to calm herself. How serene Bēltani seemed. She was wrong to feel nervous.

They sat down on the cushions together. Iltani quickly scanned the script on the tablet Bēltani gave her. She recognized the story immediately. It was one *Abu* had read to her many times. She had even seen the story performed once in honor of the New Year's festival. The tablet in her hands told of the ancient dispute between the twin sisters Lahar–Sheep, and Ashnan–Grain, divinely created to bring herd animals and grain to humankind and the gods. In the end, Ashnan was declared the more important sister.

Iltani began to read:

Ashnan (grain) called out to Lahar (sheep):
"Sister, I am your better; I take precedence over you. I am the gift of the gods to mankind. I produce bread, beer, and the beer dough. Mine is the center of each banquet.
"How can you rival me? Answer, what is your reply!"

Thereupon Lahar (sheep) answered Ashnan (grain): *"My sister, whatever are you saying? AN, King of all the gods, brought me to earth from the sacred-most place, and all the yarns of kingship, belong to me. Mine is the cloth of white wool worn by the King rejoicing on his throne. When the priests conclude their purification, they are bathed and dressed in me, my wool. I walk beside them to the holy feast.*
"Answer me what you can reply!"

Then Enki spoke to Enlil: *"Father Enlil, Sheep and Grain, Lahar and Ashnan should stand together as sisters. . . But let Ashnan (grain) be the greater of the two. Let Lahar fall on her knees before Ashnan and kiss her feet. From sunrise till sunset, may the name of Ashnan be praised. . ."*

"What a lovely reading voice you have, my dear. So clear, and yet gentle," Bēltani observed.

As Iltani reached the last line of the poem, she felt Bēltani's hand on her hair. She tried to turn around, but Bēltani's hand held her in place.

"Don't move, you have something stuck in your hair, a small twig. There, I took it out."

But Bēltani's hand moved slowly down her long dark hair and Iltani sat still as a statue for fear of offending her.

"This has been a treat and I will tell your teacher so. I look forward to our next meeting. My servant will see you home."

Bēltani summoned the servant.

"Wait, I almost forgot, a small gift for reading so well." From the shelf above her she took a delicate blue phial.

"Smell the oil, isn't it marvelous? All the way from the land of the Nile," she said, placing the phial in Iltani's hands.

"I cannot accept such a gift just for reading to you," Iltani protested.

"It is merely a small token of my appreciation. You can repay me by rubbing it on your skin next time you come to read for me," she said.

The words sounded peremptory and Iltani felt more uncomfortable than ever.

"Thank you for the oil," she replied, and turned to leave.

* * *

"I cannot wait to be away from here," Tabbija said one afternoon as they sat together in Iltani's room.

"But how will you live? Will you receive your inheritance? What about the family lands?" asked Iltani.

"I plan to be a midwife. Kunutum has been teaching me about herbs, and I still remember much that I learned from my *Abu* at home. Several times in secret I accompanied a midwife on her rounds outside the *gagû*. Once I, once we are settled," she corrected herself, smiling radiantly, "and people hear that a good midwife with a decent knowledge of herbs lives among them, I'm sure I will be much in demand."

Iltani was silent, withdrawn.

"Don't worry about me. I'll be fine. I truly believe it. I don't care if I have to work from morning till night. What more do I need than to be with the man I love? Certainly not to remain here, trapped in the life of a respectable *nadītu*," she added bitterly.

Iltani wanted to explain that it was not only Tabbija's future she was worried about, but the strange encounter with Bēltani. Was it her imagination or did this woman desire something other than her services as a scribe? But she kept these thoughts to herself.

* * *

One evening as Iltani came home from another lesson with Amat-Mamu, she recognized Kunutum in the courtyard, hastily preparing a potion of garden herbs.

"Amat-Šamaš is quite unwell. Her fever is rising. Go in to her, your company will lift her spirits."

Iltani entered Amat-Šamaš's room. She found her aunt sitting on her mattress, leaning her weakened frame against the cushions. She had lost so much weight her cheekbones protruded. The black rings under her eyes accentuated the pallor of her face. She was declining fast.

"Come Iltani, sit with me, I need to talk to you," she said feebly.

Iltani moved close to her aunt so she could hear her more clearly.

"I see you have learned your way around the *gagû*. You have a good friend within these walls, something to cultivate and cherish. You are on your way to becoming a scribe, just as you have always dreamed. Your *Abu* will leave you a good inheritance, and in time you will inherit my property as well. Listen Iltani, I know I have been distant."

Iltani was about to interrupt her, but Amat-Šamaš held up her hand.

"Please, my strength is dwindling and I wish to tell you something. I have been cold not for lack of affection. I have grown to love you very much. You are so bright and good. You warm my heart. But I have been keeping a secret from you."

Amat-Šamaš stopped. She could not speak anymore, the pain consumed her. She closed her eyes.

"Kunutum!" Iltani shouted. "Come quickly! What is wrong with her?" Iltani asked in panic. "What should I do?"

Kunutum touched Amat-Šamaš's forehead and cheeks. "She is burning up. We have to get the fever down. Quick, bring me some cloths and the water jug from the courtyard, and send Mattaki to fetch more water from the canal."

Iltani ran out to call Mattaki and carried the water jug back to Amat-Šamaš's room. Kunutum pushed away the cushions and lay her sick friend straight down on the mattress. She took a large cloth soaked in water and wrapped it around Amat-Šamaš.

"Take this," she said, handing Iltani a smaller cloth. "Wipe her face and brow with it, gently. I will run home for some special herbs. Keep her as cool as possible."

Iltani was overcome with fear. *Ummu* had told her about the babies she had lost to fever before Iltani was born. Iltani did not want to lose her aunt now that she knew and loved her. And what was she about to tell her?

Amat-Šamaš mumbled something. "What is it?" Iltani mover closer, her ear almost touching her.

"I am so happy you are here with me," she said. Iltani touched her forehead again. It seemed a little cooler.

By the time Kunutum returned, Amat-Šamaš's fever had gone down somewhat and she was semi-conscious. Kunutum boiled water and mixed in the herbs she had brought in her pouch. As soon as it cooled down, she slowly dripped the liquid into Amat-Šamaš's mouth.

When Amat-Šamaš fell into a deep sleep, Kunutum told Iltani to go rest. They would alternate that night, keeping watch over Amat-Šamaš, and Kunutum would take the first shift.

Just before the sunrise, Kunutum woke Iltani. Iltani forced herself up and hurried to Amat-Šamaš's side. Kunutum gave her something warm to drink and lay down on the far side of the room. A small oil lamp was burning, shedding just enough light for Iltani to see Amat-Šamaš's face and the contours of her body. She looked peaceful.

Iltani sat on a cushion and covered herself with a blanket. It was cold.

* * *

The first rays of light streamed into the room. "Iltani." She heard a low whisper. She had fallen asleep, sitting on the cushion.

She looked at Amat-Šamaš's face. Her eyes were open and she seemed to smile. Iltani turned to look at Kunutum who was still sleeping.

"Iltani my dear girl," she said quietly. "Your presence here brought back something from my past, long before I came to the *gagû*. Something very painful. One day I may tell you if you wish. But now, I do not fear the past anymore. I want you to know that you have made me happy. Thank you for your loving care."

Iltani reached over and kissed her aunt gently on the cheek, thanking the gods for her improvement after the long vigil.

* * *

Sounds of morning grew louder as the sun began its climb. Iltani hurried out bearing offerings for the gods, grateful that her aunt had survived the night.

On the way, she remembered Bēltani. She shuddered at the thought and tried hard to dismiss it. The main thing now was her aunt's recovery.

Chapter 9

ILTANI WAS ON HER WAY TO SEE TABBIJA. She had nursed her aunt for over three days, but since Amat-Šamaš was feeling better now and Kunutum was there to look after her, she allowed herself a well-deserved break.

She thought about the change she had seen. It was astonishing. In the process of her recovery, Amat-Šamaš seemed to become kinder and more trusting. Iltani felt she welcomed her company. At one point, Iltani almost asked her aunt about the secret she had rambled on about in her delirium, but fearing that she would turn distant again, or angry, Iltani let it drop.

* * *

The moment Iltani entered Tabbija's courtyard, she knew something was wrong. She hurried to her friend's room and found her sitting on the floor, eyes red and swollen, holding a cloth and a large bowl of water.

"What's wrong?" Iltani asked as she kneeled beside her friend. "And what is that stench?" She looked around for the source, disgusted.

"I am in serious trouble," Tabbija answered in fear.

"Tell me what it is and let me help you," Iltani said, holding her breath.

"Soon I will be leaving the *gagû*," Tabbija said.

"But why?" Iltani asked her.

"It will start to show," said Tabbija, arching her back.

Iltani had no idea what Tabbija meant. And why was she smiling now?

"Are you under some kind of spell? Shall I call a sorceress?"

"Quick, move," Tabbija ran outside to vomit in the courtyard.

"That is the terrible stench I smelled. Oh no, by Šamaš and Aja, you are ill. Don't worry, Tabbija. I will send a message to your *Abu*. He is a good doctor and he will not let you die and leave the *gagû*!" said Iltani.

"Die?" asked Tabbija quizzically. "I am not going to die. I have to leave the *gagû* because I am with child. I will not be able to hide it for long. See? My belly is swelling," she whispered.

"You are with child?" Iltani was baffled. "But a *nadītu* is not allowed to be with a man! I assumed you would wait, after you leave."

Tabbija pulled Iltani back into the room.

"Look Iltani. I did not want to wait. It is a natural part of the love between a man and a woman. I have used special herbs as contraception for many months now, but I guess they failed. I am not sad I am pregnant, just scared of what will be. All this happened too soon. . ."

"What will you do now?" Iltani asked stunned by this information.

"Liwira-ana-ilim will try to find a position in a village near Babylon. There is a need for good workers in the area we have heard, and he has plenty of experience. We will run away together. Liwira-ana-ilim will tell them that his wife is with child and that she is a midwife. Perhaps that will help. My family must not know. Say nothing to them, I beg you, Iltani. They may be harassed by the overseer of the *gagû*. Once I am safely settled, I will send a message that I am married and safe. Promise me you will not tell anyone, Iltani, please."

"I promise."

Iltani was too overwhelmed to absorb what she had heard. All she could think about was that her friend, her only friend in the *gagû*, was leaving her. Who would she confide in now?

She wanted to tell Tabbija about the strange feeling she had about Bēltani, but she never got around to it. Tabbija vomited again and then needed to rest. When her friend had fallen asleep, she quietly left the room and returned home, mulling over the events of the last few days.

* * *

A few days later, Iltani sat in her room practicing the signs, pronouncing them aloud. Over and over she pressed the stylus into the moist clay till her hands became sore and blistered. It took her mind off the shocking meeting with Tabbija. She would look in on her later in the day, she decided.

Iltani was gratified to see her aunt feeling so much better she could get around the *gagû* and even walk to the temple with Mattaki.

"Iltani, are you there?" She heard a voice call from the courtyard.

"I am Bēltani's servant and she sent me to bring you to her, now."

"Right now?"

"Yes, she awaits you. She hopes you will use the perfumed oil she gave you. I will wait here."

Iltani did not want to go, but what excuse could she give? Her aunt was well again, as everyone knew, and she couldn't possibly lie about having a lesson with Amat-Mamu since Bēltani had no doubt spoken with her.

"All right, I will get ready now," she said turning back to her room. She removed her upper garment and unplugged the small phial. She sprinkled the oil on her skin and rubbed it in. The smell was sweet and flowery.

* * *

"There you are, my sister, thank you for coming," Bēltani said, greeting Iltani warmly, touching her shoulder.

"I hear your aunt was ill. I hope she is feeling better now. I prayed for her at the temple this morning."

"She is feeling a little better, thought she is still very feeble," Iltani explained.

"Ah, you used the oil I gave you. Isn't it lovely? You smell so sweet," Bēltani said with a honeyed voice, changing the subject.

"Yes thank you, it is a lovely smell."

"Come, I have a beautiful poem for you to read today. Never mind the difficult passages. Just take your time. Perhaps we can discuss it afterward." Bēltani led her to the cushions.

"That would be nice. *Abu* and I used to talk about poems together," Iltani said.

She picked up the tablet and Bēltani leaned closer, as if to read with her.

Iltani scanned the signs. They did not appear too difficult. She began to read aloud:

"O! What sweet things you do to me,
My dear sweet one.
Your taste is sweet as honey!
Let us enjoy your charms and sweetness,
over and over again!
O! Lad, What sweet things you do to me,
my sweet dear one,
Give me that which is honey-sweet!
Pour your sweetness into me;
O press it there
Like flour in a measuring cup
O pound it, pound it there for me!
Like flour in the
measuring cup!"

Iltani was so absorbed with the reading, so careful not to mistake the signs that she did not even notice Bēltani sniffing her neck and shoulders.

"How beautiful, how sensual," Bēltani said when Iltani finished reading. "Don't you agree?"

"Yes, beautiful," Iltani muttered. She felt a growing unease in Bēltani's presence. "I think I should go now." She stood up.

"Before you go, I want to give you this beautiful cloth, in return for your beautiful reading. The yarn comes all the way from Nippur. I had my best weavers make this for you. Come. My servant will take your measurements and sew a garment for you. Take off your over dress," she said as she left the room.

Reluctantly she took off her overdress and stood shivering in her light shift.

Bēltani returned carrying a length of cloth, followed by her servant. The servant wrapped the cloth around Iltani. It felt soft.

"Yes, how well this suits you," she said. "The red and purple stripes, the shimmering yellow threads woven into the cotton." The servant stuck needles in the cloth to hold it in place. "There," she said, "now take it off, but mind the needles."

"Leave us now," Bēltani ordered the servant with some impatience.

"It is beautiful, yes," Bēltani said, moving closer to Iltani. "It falls delightfully around your shoulders. Let me see the back." She walked around Iltani, slowly stroking her.

Iltani froze. Bēltani's hand meandered over her shoulders and down her back to her buttocks.

"The cloth is so soft, so soft. . ." she now stood facing Iltani.

"Come let me help you take off the dress, so you won't be pricked by the needles."

"I can do it myself," Iltani protested.

"Come, come, Iltani, all those needles. Let me help you, just hold still." Bēltani was watching her like a tiger.

Slowly she undid the upper cloth, lightly brushing Iltani's breasts.

"How delicate you are. Your sweetness arouses my desire for the pleasures we read about in the poem. Let me show you, let me guide you in the art of pleasure. I will be very gentle, you will enjoy it." She leaned in and kissed her gently on the lips, her fingers stroking through her hair.

Iltani's body turned to stone, but her mind was racing. She understood; Bēltani wanted of her what the woman in the poem wanted of the man. That is why she had asked her to read it.

She felt Bēltani's hand slide down her neck and touch her breast, lifting her tunic, her hand slid between her legs.

"No!" Iltani heard herself shout. "I don't like this!" She stepped back and tripped over the cloth, staring fearfully at Bēltani.

"I am very powerful, you know. Those who are my friends enjoy many benefits in the *gagû*, and outside too. Better to be in my favor then to be counted among my adversaries," she added calmly.

"I am not your adversary, but what you want is not . . . is not right for me. I never wanted to know a man, or a woman in such a way as described in the poem. My only true desire ever was to become a scribe."

Bēltani looked unperturbed. She smiled calmly at Iltani. "This is all a misunderstanding. I merely offered you a pleasure I am sure you have never experienced before," she said in a sweet voice. "I thought you liked me. After all, you did accept my precious gifts and put on that delicious smelling oil for me. Go, go home to your tablets. You may change your mind one day soon and I will welcome you, sweet, pure woman."

Bēltani left the room. Iltani quickly dressed herself and hurried out of the house.

Sometime later Bēltani called her servant. "Go fetch Amat-Mamu!" she yelled angrily. "I will teach her to resist me. She will beg me to take her back."

* * *

On her way home Iltani stopped at the bathhouse. She felt sullied and confused. Should she tell her aunt, she wondered, shivering. Would Amat-Šamaš believe her? But Iltani did not want to add to her worries. Her aunt was so weak. She would pray for Aja's protection and help. She needed help. Just as she was approaching home she saw Kunutum running towards her.

"Hurry, your aunt is sick again. Where have you been?"

A group of women stood by the entrance to the courtyard.

"What has happened?" Iltani asked in alarm.

"Your aunt has a high fever. She's calling for you."

Iltani ran in to her aunt's room.

"I am so sorry," she kneeled and took Amat-Šamaš's hand.

"Iltani my dearest, I feel there is not much time left," she whispered, and then looked past Iltani into the air.

Her body was burning. Iltani changed the wet cloth to cool her down.

"Please Iltani, send everyone away. I need to talk to you," Amat-Šamaš said.

Iltani quickly obeyed.

"I must tell you the secret I have kept so long. So you'll understand. There are some in the world who mistreat the young and the weak. They will not only hurt you, they will make you think it was your fault, or find a way to frighten you into doing what they want." Amat-Šamaš paused. Iltani wiped her brow.

"I come from a poor family, that much you know. We lived in the south, in the city of Ur. *Abu* and my brothers worked the fields around the temple of Nanna, and *Ummu* sold the cloth she wove at home. I stayed home with *Ummu* and helped her with the cooking and the weaving.

"We were a happy family. Friends and neighbors would often visit us in the evenings, bringing food and drink to share, and we would eat together and tell stories about the gods and heroes and *Abu* would sing and play the lyre. But then, when I turned fourteen, everything changed. My uncle, *Abu's* youngest brother, came to live with us. He was a laggard, too lazy to work. He made *Abu's* blood boil. 'Go, get out, do some work!' *Abu* would shout at him. 'I can't provide for you—I barely have enough for my own children!' But it was no use. Uncle idled around the house. He brought no fruit or barley. And then, one day while my mother was selling cloth in the *kārum* of Ur, Uncle found me playing in the courtyard.

"He was holding a sickle in his hands, trying to tie it to a handle made of reeds. He asked me to help him, to hold the sickle while he tied it. I was young and trusting. How eagerly I ran to help him. When the sickle was repaired he asked me to go with him to the room where we slept at night. And there he threw me on the floor and held the sickle to my face. He said that if I screamed he would kill me. Next thing I knew he was kissing me and touching my breasts. I was ashamed, I was afraid to cry out. Then he lifted my dress and I began to scream but he put his hand over my mouth. I couldn't breathe. He lay on top of me and pried my legs open. He told me I was a good little virgin, an honor and a pleasure for him. And then I felt a terrible pain between my legs as he forced me again and again. I fainted. When I woke up he was washing me off. I shouted for help but he covered my mouth again and told me that he loved me and that he had done me a kindness. He warned me that if I dared tell my parents he would kill them and sell me as a slave. I was so frightened I believed him. A man who violated his niece would have no qualms about killing a brother and his family. So I did not tell *Ummu* and *Abu* and my life became unbearable. He violated me many times, after that, whenever he had a chance, always forcefully and always cleaned me up afterwards.

"After a while my parents noticed that something was wrong. One day *Ummu* took me to a midwife who announced that I was pregnant. *Abu* nearly murdered Uncle, who fled from Ur and we never heard from him again. Just before my baby was born, my family moved to a small village outside of Babylon where *Abu* and my brothers worked the fields for a rich landowner. *Ummu* and *Abu* thought it would be best for me to leave the child in their care, once it was born. They would raise her as their own and I would work as a *nadītu*'s servant. I had no idea what a *nadītu* was, but I was glad to leave the child with them. I could not bear to look at it; the pain and shame were so great." She stopped, took a deep breath and stared at Iltani. "That child is your mother."

Iltani was too shocked to move. Her poor aunt, then she realized, Amat-Šamaš was her grandmother.

Amat-Šamaš breathed heavily. "Iltani, come closer. I did not like your *Ummu* because she reminded me of what happened. But when she reached womanhood, I gave her a dowry, thanks to the *nadītu* who adopted me. This is what made it possible for her to marry your *Abu* and secure her future."

Iltani listened, scarcely comprehending.

"When you entered the *gagû*, it was hard for me. The memories I had buried so long rose to the surface. But these months with you here brought me happiness. When I go to the land of the dead, I will go in peace. I helped your *Ummu* marry well and you are here in the safety of the *gagû*. My child, I love you," she said and kissed Iltani's hand.

Iltani burst into tears. She embraced Amat-Šamaš and felt her feverish body.

"I love you too, Amat-Šamaš. You must get well. You must! Don't leave me."

Kunutum hurried to her side with a special remedy, but Amat-Šamaš was already unconscious and her hand lay limp and cold in Iltani's hand.

Kunutum tried to wake Amat-Šamaš, but to no avail. Iltani cried out in pain. She did not move from Amat-Šamaš' side. Kunutum and Mattaki changed Amat-Šamaš's sheets, moistened her lips, washed her face gently, but nothing helped.

Next morning, as the sun rose over the *gagû*, the last days in the month of Simanu, Amat-Šamaš breathed her last.

Chapter 10

"MY DEAR CHILD, IT IS TIME. Three days have passed now and you must set your aunt's spirit free."

Iltani looked at Mattaki. She understood. Slowly, stiffly, she turned towards the small clay statue beside the shrouded body of Amat-Šamaš.

"Come, Iltani, everyone is waiting—your family, the priests, the wailing women."

Mattaki took Iltani's hands and helped her to her feet.

"I have packed food and beer and some oil for your aunt," Mattaki said. "And there is a special bead necklace I want to send with her. You too must bring gifts."

"For Amat-Šamaš?" Iltani asked in a daze.

"Yes, for her life in the world below."

"Of course," Iltani comprehended at last. "Yes, I will bring something."

* * *

Iltani seemed to have no will of her own. She had never known the pain of losing a loved one before. She breathed with difficulty.

"Here drink this." She heard Kunutum's voice, hoarse with mourning. She had brought Iltani a potion to comfort her and give her strength.

Four strong temple-servants carried the bier on which Amat-Šamaš's corpse lay. Iltani walked behind them, supported by Mattaki and Kunutum, followed by a long line of *nadītu*, among them Tabbija. Outside the *gagû*, Iltani's family waited to join the funeral procession. The wailing women ululated eerily, beating their chests and tearing at their hair.

Iltani paid no attention. Catching sight of *Abu* and *Ummu* she fell into their arms and clasped them with all her might.

As the servants laid Amat-Šamaš's corpse in the earth, howling and lamenting broke out on every hand and the wailers continued to ululate and beat their chests. Kunutum approached the burial pit of her friend and dropped a few small jars and a loaf of bread inside it. *Ummu* had brought a special cake which she placed in the pit. One by one, people approached and placed their gifts on the corpse until it was almost entirely covered.

The priest approached Iltani and said, "The spirit of Amat-Šamaš must now be set free."

Iltani kneeled beside the pit and lodged her gifts there—fragrant oil, food, beer, and her favorite writing stylus. Amat-Šamaš's contours were visible through the shrouds.

The priest signaled to Iltani. "*Spirit, you are free,*" Iltani recited the incantation that would allow Amat-Šamaš's body to pass over to the land of the dead.

The crowd backed away from the pit and the servants began to cover the shrouded corpse with soil and stones.

As through a thick blanket, Iltani heard the mumblings of consolers, and felt her body was being hugged by many people. After a while, she found herself alone at the graveside. A light breeze ruffled Iltani's hair and dress; a shiver went through her. The soil that covered the body of Amat-Šamaš, Iltani mused, would also bury the secrets they shared.

"Iltani, my child," she heard *Abu* say as he hugged her tightly. "It is sad that we must meet under these circumstances. This must be hard for you, but they will let you out of the *gagû* now to mourn with us at home. Come, we will help you carry the belongings you will need for a week and the votive statue, guardian of Amat-Šamaš spirit."

"*Abu*, I have missed you so much," was all Iltani was able to say as she clasped his arm.

She briefly had to return to the *gagû*. Mattaki helped her pack for a few days, and then accompanied her to her childhood home.

Iltani, seeing Sin-rēmēni again, was overwhelmed with love for him. He held onto her and would not let her go. He told her that Shima-ahati had decided to leave shortly after Iltani's departure, an unpleasant surprise for everyone in the family. Iltani felt an ache in her heart. Had she remained at home, would Shima-ahati have stayed on? She was a servant, not a slave, and had the right to leave whenever she wanted, but Iltani missed her presence in the house. She tried to imagine her, happy in old age wherever she was.

"Iltani, did you hear?" said Sin-rēmēni. "I now go to the É-DUBBA. *Abu* decided that I should. But I do not like it there at all. I cannot remember any of the signs and I mix them up all the time. I have been whipped a few times already."

"Little brother, the beginning is always hardest, and in time you will memorize the signs, do not worry," said Iltani. But she was abstracted, distressed. Her thoughts wandered back to Amat-Šamaš's secrets, her illness and her death. And then to the horrid encounter with Bēltani.

Every morning Iltani recited prayers for the spirit of Amat-Šamaš and set bowls of food and water before the statue. She was obliged to perform this rite every day from now on as the heir of the dead woman. It was usually the duty of the child of the deceased or of the parents, if their child died, but as *nadītu* did not bear children, the duty reverted to their adopted *nadītu*.

"But wait," she thought and froze, Amat-Šamaš did have a child; *Ummu* was her child. If *Ummu* failed to provide for the spirit, it was liable to become angered and come to haunt *Ummu*. She looked around at the comforters. There was an invisible wall around her, she felt, a wall of secrets. Should she break it down? Could she? Iltani closed her eyes and prayed to Šamaš and Aja for guidance. When she opened her eyes again, she saw *Ummu* clearing away what remained of the food. No, Iltani herself would tend Amat-Šamaš's spirit, she would not break that wall of secrets, and cause pain and perhaps shame to her mother and her entire family. The secrets would stay buried forevermore.

* * *

"Amat-Šamaš was very ill, it is a great mercy that she no longer suffers," *Abu* said. "At least she had you there in her last days; you must have been a solace to her. Did you get along well?"

"Not at first, but in time we did." Iltani rested her head on *Abu*'s shoulder. "I missed you so much, you and *Ummu* and Sin-rēmēni."

The pain she felt at losing Amat-Šamaš, Bēltani's hounding, and the imminent departure of her only friend from the *gagû* made tears roll down her cheeks.

She sobbed like a child in *Abu*'s arms. She dreaded the moment of leaving home again. Parting was much harder this time, knowing what lay ahead for her. Isolation, loneliness, and confrontations with Bēltani. The only ray of light there—her scribal lessons that would soon continue.

The week went by very fast and it was Iltani's last day at home. She had not washed or changed her clothes in keeping with mourning customs. Most of the time she had kept quietly to herself or chatted with Sin-rēmēni and stroked Humbaba, who loved to cuddle next to her. She was not the same girl she had been six months before. The *gagû* did not only represent an honorable status anymore, but rather a place of passage to maturity.

* * *

"You will have to learn how to manage your inheritance now," Mattaki said, counseling Iltani a few days

after her return to the *gagû*. "As the new owner of Amat-
Šamaš's properties."

"*Abu* sees to all my needs; food, clothing, oil,
everything."

"Yes, but you have inherited much land which has
been leased out. The leaseholder may cheat you if you are
not on guard. You are a grown woman now, not a child.
You must consider your future. Not many *nadītu* are as
fortunate as you are. Read the tablet with your aunt's
bequest so you will know what is yours by right."

"Yes, you are right." Iltani answered slowly,
remembering the *nadītu* she had seen with Amat-Mamu after
the beating. "Where are the tables kept?"

"Ask the UGULA. They are usually stored next to the
UGULA's chambers in the House of Aja, though some
nadītu prefer to keep them at home. Your aunt did not keep
her tablets here," Mattaki said.

"All right, I will go look later," Iltani agreed reluctantly.

"There is one more thing Iltani," said Mattaki. "I am
getting too old to work here. It is time for my children to
take care of me. I stayed with your aunt longer then I
should have. It has become too tiring for me. You should
start looking for a new servant."

"But Mattaki, I need you," Iltani said in dismay. "Please
don't leave me now!"

"I am very sorry, Iltani." Mattaki said compassionately.
"You know how fond I am of you and how happy I was to
work for your noble aunt. I must leave. But not until the
end of Âbu, so you will have a few months to hire a new
servant, enough time for me to teach her the work too, if
you wish. You should ask the priest in the Šamaš-temple to
find a servant for you. They often have knowledge of
women who are looking for work. Believe me, Iltani, it is
for the best. Put the past behind you. You are young, you
will soon be a scribe, you have your aunt's fortune. I will

soon go to my fate. It is fitting that I spend my last days among my children and grandchildren."

"I understand," said Iltani, though her heart was in confusion. Why were all these things happening to her at the same time? Amat-Šamaš's death, the vileness of Bēltani, Tabbija's coming departure, and now Mattaki's announcement. Had she sinned against the gods? Were her offerings remiss?

* * *

The UGULA's impatience with the affairs of the *nadītu* had reached a new peak. To be installed in one of the splendid chambers of Hammurabi's palace, away from this *gagû*, that was what he hankered for.

"What is it?" the UGULA asked harshly, his eyes sullen. "What do you need?"

"I would like to see the records left by my aunt, Amat-Šamaš." Her grandmother, actually, Iltani thought with a shiver. "She died recently, as you know, and I am her heir. It is necessary for me to read her bequest," said Iltani.

"That is not my responsibility," the UGULA said. "Talk to the scribe in charge of the archive, the *ṭupšarru rabû*. Did no one tell you? Don't you *nadītu* ever speak to one another? What do you do all day?"

"I am sorry to have troubled you. I will seek out the *ṭupšarru rabû*," she said. Iltani felt belittled. No, no one had told her. She might have asked Kunutum. She left his chamber, hoping the scribe would be friendlier and more accommodating.

* * *

"Yes, of course I can help you," said the old scribe calmly. He stood bowed over his cane in the corridor, bald and bright-eyed, with a short white beard that framed his wrinkled face. He smiled at Iltani, radiating kindness and she sighed with relief.

"Your aunt Amat-Šamaš—yes, she had various problems as I recall; a lawsuit to answer, ill-health," he said, signaling her to follow him into a large adjoining room.

The room was crowded with reed-baskets and heavy wooden shelves lined with clay tablets, hundreds of them. Iltani glanced around in awe. How could the scribe find anything amongst so many tablets? she wondered.

"I have worked here since I finished studying at the É-DUBBA, first as a simple scribe and later I became the *ṭupšarru rabû*, responsible for this archive. I am acquainted with almost all the *nadītu*. Wait here, I'll find your aunt's tablet."

Iltani watched the old scribe opening lids, deftly flipping through the tablets and reading a few lines of each before disappearing behind some shelves.

"Here it is," he called. "Come help me carry the basket."

They pushed the heavy reed-basket to the middle of the room where there was more space and sunlight filtering in through the door.

"I see Amat-Šamaš has quite a few tablets. Should I read them for you?"

"I would be grateful. Then I will decide if to take any home."

The scribe picked up one of the tablets and scanned the text.

"It says here that Amat-Šamaš bought land with her ring money. This is the original deed. You will need this tablet to prove ownership and to sell or bequeath the property if you so wish," said the old scribe. He began to read aloud to Iltani. First came a description of the field and then the terms of the transaction.

"Amat-Šamaš the nadītu of Šamaš, has bought a field;

three acres wide in Kār-Šamaš district, adjacent to the field of Šamaš-rabi, and adjacent to the field of Bēlšunu, bordering on the canal.

She bought the field with her 'ring-money' from Waqatum the nadītu of Šamaš.

She paid the full price in silver.

Her heart is satisfied, the transaction is completed.

In future neither party will sue the other.

By Šamaš, Aja Marduk and Hammurabi the King they have sworn."

"And below this appear the names of eight witnesses and the date of the deed," concluded the scribe.

"What do the other tablets say?" Iltani asked.

"This one is about leasing your field and the price you should get for it." The old scribe read the tablet aloud.

"And this one," he said, pointing to a large tablet, "is a trial record. The brothers of the *nadītu* who adopted *Amat-Šamaš* accused her of falsifying the will. They sued your aunt but she won the trial and kept the property.

"I may as well leave the tablets with you. They are probably safer here."

"Yes, that is what this house is for. Tablets in the keeping of *nadītu* sometimes get lost. Here we find everything sooner or later."

"Thank you," Iltani said.

"If you should ever need my assistance again, for any reason at all, please come to me," the old scribe said and smiled at her, revealing a mouth with very few teeth.

"I will. May *Šamaš* reward you for all your help, *ṭupšarru rabû*," she said. How much nicer he was than the UGULA. His kindness reminded her of *Abu*.

* * *

"What do you mean, you cannot teach me anymore?" Iltani realized she was fairly screaming at Amat-Mamu.

"Forgive me, I did not intend to raise my voice," she said immediately.

"I have no time, as I already explained to your *Abu*. There is nothing to be done about it. I must ask you to leave now."

"Just like that? But why?" Iltani was distraught. Her main reason for becoming a *nadītu*, the only reason she had been able to cope with all that had befallen her of later, was evaporating like a splash of water on parched soil of the summer. "Is it a question of money? I am sure *Abu* would be willing to pay you more."

Amat-Mamu, who usually stood proud and erect, looking her straight in the eye, seemed shrunken and evasive somehow.

"I am such a hard-working pupil and you are a superlative teacher," Iltani tried to soften the harsh decree.

But Amat-Mamu bowed her head and turned away. "You must leave at once. There is nothing more to say," she replied, leaving Iltani alone in the room.

Iltani was stunned; her first lesson since Amat-Šamaš's funeral, the one ray of light in these dark days, was not to be. But why? What made Amat-Mamu change her mind about teaching her?

Disconsolate, bewildered, Iltani walked out the door. She wandered aimlessly around the *gagû* and it was nearly dark by the time she found herself in Tabbija's courtyard. She found her friend preparing dinner.

"Iltani! What happened? You look as though you have seen a demon." Tabbija jumped up to hug her.

"I do not understand!" said Iltani, shaking her head from side to side. "Amat-Mamu dismissed me! She will no longer teach me."

"Amat-Mamu?" Tabbija asked in surprise. "But why? What reason did she give you?"

"No time for me, that is all she would say. Oh, Tabbija!" Iltani moaned. "I think the gods must be angry

97

with me. So many bad things have happened since I entered the *gagû*."

"Nonsense, there must be some explanation for this. Your aunt had been ailing for a long time; fate has taken her where she will not suffer anymore. But Amat-Mamu, that is unclear. Did you have a quarrel with her?"

"No, and I never disobeyed her. I worked hard and. . ." Of course, it was Bēltani, Iltani realized in shock.

"What is it, Iltani?" Tabbija asked.

Iltani looked intently at her friend. The time had come to tell the only person she trusted about Bēltani. "I have to tell you a secret, but you must promise not to tell anyone, or to judge me."

"I won't if you won't," Tabbija stroked her belly with a radiant smile. "Soon I will be gone, Iltani. Reveal what is in your heart and you will see what a relief it is to trust someone with your secrets."

Iltani paced in the room. She picked up the water jug and drank from it, then splashed her face and dried it with her dress.

"You asked if I had a quarrel with Amat-Mamu. I did not. But I had a nasty disagreement with Bēltani."

"What kind of disagreement?" Tabbija raised her eyebrows.

"Well, she . . . ah, " Iltani stuttered. "Bēltani wanted me to become her lover."

"By Šamaš, Aja and Marduk. So it is true," Tabbija said in disbelief.

"What is?" Iltani was afraid her secret had spread. "What have you heard about me?"

"About you? Nothing. But there are rumors about Bēltani, that she likes women and finds ways of making them do what she wants."

"I think it is Bēltani who is behind this. She must have coerced Amat-Mamu to stop teaching me. Amat-Mamu herself told me once that Bēltani is her most important patron and that she is somehow indebted to her."

"This is serious," Tabbija replied, shaking her head with dismay.

"What should I do? Complain to the UGULA?"

"No, never that. Given Bēltani's money and connections, she no doubt has power over the UGULA. He will not help you unless you approach him with the Princess. It was she who helped me when Liwira-ana-ilim was taken. If I were you, I would tell no one. Rumor has it that some years ago a young *nadītu* complained to everyone about Bēltani—the Šamaš-priest, the gate-keeper and the previous UGULA."

"And what happened then?" Iltani asked.

"A few months later she was found dead in her room," Tabbija whispered.

"Dead? You mean Bēltani killed her?" Iltani said in horror.

"No. The rumors say that Bēltani managed to impoverish her family somehow and the rest is unclear. She died that winter."

Iltani was mortified. "You mean I must become her lover or die?"

"No, of course not. Just keep your distance from Bēltani and say nothing. If she ordered Amat-Mamu not to teach you anymore, that is that. Find another way to become a scribe. There must be another way for you."

"But she is the only female scribe in the *gagû*, the rest are men. Would they teach me?"

"I do not know," Tabbija said, "but whatever you do, be careful, steer clear of Bēltani."

* * *

"We have an understanding then? You are sure this is within your power?" asked the UGULA.

"I assure you that will not be a problem," said Bēltani, smiling maliciously. "By next winter you will be in Babylon, serving in the royal temple. Until then you must abide by my request. If you rule your staff with rigor, they will obey."

"I will see to that," answered the UGULA, noting Bēltani's tone of disdain, but he did not care.

The moment she had left his chamber, he smiled from ear to ear. Soon, next winter, he would be installed in Babylon. This was a day to celebrate.

Chapter 11

IT WAS STILL RATHER HOT for the month of Ulûlu. Everywhere people of Sippar were repairing the damages their houses suffered during the winter, preparing for the next cold season, reconstructing the roofs of their houses, fortifying and painting the clay-brick walls, dredging silt from the drinking canals. Outside the city, farmers sowed their irrigated fields with chickpeas.

At this time of year, the city moved slowly. Streets were empty on hot afternoons, but the river was full of laughing children and their mothers.

* * *

Iltani lay on her mattress, staring at the wall. For days she had hardly eaten or stirred from the house. After Mattaki left, Iltani had hired no one to take her place. She had stopped going to the bathhouse, even after her monthly bleeding. Her hair was so grimy it had a noisome smell. The pantry stood empty, the courtyard forsaken.

Ummu said she was born in the month of Ulûlu, so by now she must have reached the age of eighteen, but what was that to her? There was nothing to get up for. Had Kunutum and Tabbija not brought water and food to her side, Iltani might have dried up and starved to death.

Tabbija came to part before leaving the *gagû*, her belly barely hidden by a loose cloak.

"Iltani, my dearest friend, you must get up and look after yourself," Tabbija said in tears.

"What for?" shrugged Iltani.

"For yourself. For your family." Tabbija raised her voice.

Iltani shrugged. "Go, my friend. Your secret is safe with me. At least one of us will lead the life she wants to."

"I am so sorry I must leave you now, but I have no choice. Soon it will be too late, I will not be able to hide my belly anymore."

"I know, sister of my heart," said Iltani.

Tabbija embraced her and promised to send a message as soon as possible from her new home. "I leave you with a heavy heart. I pray that I will see you well again someday."

* * *

A few days after Tabbija vanished from the *gagû*, the UGULA and the priests came by to question Iltani. She told them she knew nothing and they left her alone. The *gagû* was in an uproar, everyone speculating about Tabbija's disappearance. The news reached her family. Her father, a respectable *asû*, was the object of gossip and scrutiny. The UGULA demanded compensation for all the offerings his daughter would have brought and three months' rent for her room in the *gagû*.

A few months later, Tabbija sent her family a message with a traveling merchant saying she was well and married to Liwira-ana-ilim. They were relieved to know she was alive and well, though shocked that she had run off with the son of a former slave. They asked the merchant where she lived, but he could not answer; he had been paid to deliver the message by another merchant and did not know Tabbija or Liwira-ana-ilim himself. Tabbija's family decided to search no further and put the distressing incident behind them.

Iltani was oblivious to the commotion in the *gagû*. She lay in her room, sleeping most of the time or staring at the wall when awake.

Kunutum saw the hopelessness in Iltani's eyes. She had seen this vacant look before in the eyes of girls who had been forced to enter the *gagû*.

"Here, drink this." Kunutum handed Iltani a cup.

"Why?" asked Iltani. "Will it change anything?"

"No, it will not bring anyone back to you, not Tabbija or Amat-Šamas. But it tastes good," she said, persuading her.

"You forget one thing, Kunutum," said Iltani. "The reason I came to the *gagû* in the first place was to learn to be a scribe. My teacher refuses to teach me now. I am bereft, destiny has betrayed me. There is nothing for me here. I am a prisoner, and it is my own fault," she added in a strange monotone voice.

"You will be in the *gagû* for the rest of your life. Is there no other way for you to learn?" asked Kunutum.

"Probably not," said Iltani, staring at her few clay tablets on the floor.

"Iltani, dear sister, I was a very good friend to your aunt," she said, stressing the word aunt, as some secrets are best never mentioned. "I know what a difficult life she led, how hard she had to work even after she became a *nadītu*. You are of her blood. I do not know how, but you must find a way to become a scribe. You are a free woman with a house and money of your own. You are not a child anymore, under the protection of your parents. You are your own mistress. Here in the *gagû* there are only two kinds of women: those who are in a permanent state of despair over their fate, to be a *nadītu*, and their existence is miserable; and those who use whatever talents they possess to enrich their lives. It is up to you to decide which type of woman you will become."

Kunutum smiled and opened her arms. Iltani hugged her with some reluctance.

"You have grieved for your aunt. Now start living. If you wish it to, the *gagû* will hold out a happy destiny," she said, embracing Iltani. "And as your friend and a healer of the sick, I can tell you that the first thing you must do is to bathe," said Kunutum, squinching her nose at the smell of her, with a smile of amusement. Iltani nodded assent.

Kunutum had brought some food, which Iltani ate without relish.

* * *

Later that night, Iltani thought about Kunutum's words. Yes, Kunutum was right; she was not a child anymore. At home she had lived an easy, sheltered life with no worries, no disappointments. She had thought it would be the same in the *gagû*, that her aunt would take care of her, that she would go on learning. She did not want to live in despair; she wanted to become a scribe. She knew Amat-Mamu would be willing to teach her again if she submitted to Bēltani's desires. Was she willing to pay such a price? "Never!" she said aloud. There had to be another way.

Iltani closed her eyes and did something she had not done in a long time. She prayed to the gods for help. She asked for a sign.

Feeling somewhat uplifted, she decided to take Kunutum's advice. First thing in the morning, after providing food and water for Amat-Šamaš's spirit, she would go to the bathhouse.

The next day, after a bath, she felt stronger. She swept the house and the courtyard, which were filthy, in a state of chaos. Then she tended the herb garden, planted by Kunutum long ago.

Later, she went to the temple to ask one of the Šamaš-priests to help her find a servant, either someone like Mattaki who would come in early and leave before the *gagû* gates were closed for the night, or a girl who would board with her. Iltani did not have a preference.

Very soon, the priest sent her a divorced woman who had returned to her father's house and had to work to support the family. Her name was Parratum. Iltani liked her and hired her on the spot. She was small and quiet. She usually stayed overnight, but sometimes, she left after dinner to see her parents. Iltani asked her about her life, her family, but Parratum was reticent, so she left her alone. Perhaps in time she would open up.

As yet, Iltani had not solved the problem of her scribal education, but every day she asked the gods for a sign. They will ultimately help me, she thought. They must.

* * *

"You are looking remarkably healthy," said Kunutum one day when she dropped by.

"Thank you. I feel a little better," she said as she loosened the soil in the herb garden. It reminded her of kneading clay.

"Are you going to talk to Amat-Mamu again? Perhaps she has changed her mind?"

"No, there is no chance of that. I will find another way," said Iltani, and as she stated the words, she believed them. In her mind, a plan began to form. She decided to ask the *ṭupšarru rabû* at the archive for help. Perhaps he would be willing to teach her.

When Iltani went to see the old *ṭupšarru rabû*, she could not find him anywhere.

"Where is the keeper of the archive, the old *ṭupšarru rabû*?" Iltani asked a young scribe, whom she found in the archive of the *gagû*.

"He is gone."

"But why?" Iltani asked astonished. "Was he ill?"

The scribe seemed uneasy about this. "No. He was simply unwilling to follow an order from the UGULA. I am the new *ṭupšarru rabû*. "

"What order was that?" asked Iltani, a dark suspicion stealing into her heart.

"That no male scribe is allowed to teach a *nadītu* of the *gagû*, something, that has always been allowed before. The UGULA decreed that any scribe who disregarded that order would be punished. The *ṭupšarru rabû* refused to comply, and said that if a *nadītu* should ask him it would be an honor to teach her. So the UGULA banished him from the *gagû*."

Iltani was downcast by this, but not surprised. Bēltani was surely involved in this turn of events, and if Iltani wished to become a scribe she knew she would have to confront her. Or else wait until the first two years were up, and then find a scribe outside the *gagû* to teach her.

* * *

Iltani had never confronted anyone before and she was apprehensive. It was her nature to compromise; she hated quarreling. But since the death of Amat-Šamaš, Kunutum's words rang in her ears. Iltani understood. Henceforth, it would be up to her. She would have to look after herself. If becoming a scribe was what she wanted, she would have to fight to become one.

She had heeded the warnings to tell no one about Bēltani, yet Bēltani had forbidden Amat-Mamu and the *gagû* scribes to teach her, that much was clear. She decided to act. She had nothing to lose. Her choice was either to become a scribe or a despairing *nadītu*.

* * *

"Iltani, what a lovely surprise, how nice of you to visit," said Bēltani.

Iltani's felt her courage drip away like beer from a crack in a jug.

"May Šamaš and Aja keep you forever healthy. I wish to thank you for the generous gifts of food you brought to the funeral."

"Ah well, bringing food was the least I could do. Your aunt was a fine *nadītu*."

It was now or never, Iltani realized; otherwise Bēltani might get the wrong idea about the visit. Attack, she urged herself, and looked Bēltani straight in the eye as she spoke: "I entreat you, Bēltani, allow Amat-Mamu or another scribe in the *gagû* to teach me again."

"Whatever makes you think I ordered Amat-Mamu, or anyone else, not to instruct you? Why, I was not even aware that Amat-Mamu had stopped teaching. What is it to me whether she teaches or not?" she answered serenely, raising her eyebrows.

Iltani was surprised by her calm reaction. "No one told me you were behind this, Bēltani. I guessed. Amat-Mamu merely said she had too much work to bother with a student, and I heard about the UGULA's new decree. I know you were furious, Bēltani, that you could not have your way with me."

Bēltani was clearly stunned and for a moment seemed to vacillate. Then her eyes narrowed on Iltani and as she raised her hand, Iltani feared that she would strike her.

"Loathsome girl!" Bēltani seized her by the shoulder. "I do not appreciate your coming here with these accusations. I merely tried to be nice to you, and this is how you repay me! Get out, leave my house at once!" Bēltani shoved her harshly.

Though Iltani was petrified, she soon regained her balance and slowly walked away. Outside in the courtyard, she swerved around and stared boldly at Bēltani. Show no fear, she urged herself.

"I am still young. I will become a scribe one day, even if I have to wait until you are old and toothless," Iltani said in a clear, strong voice. "I am not afraid of you."

As soon as she was out of earshot, too far away to be seen by Bēltani, Iltani crouched down. Her small frame shook so violently she could scarcely walk. She leaned against a wall. She had fought her first fight. Her words were bound to have consequences, but she did not care. She thanked the gods for giving her the strength to confront Bēltani. She did not really expect Amat-Mamu to teach her again, but the act of fighting back restored her hope and made her feel stronger, able to stand on her own two feet.

* * *

It was Arahsamna, beginning autumn, and Iltani had heard nothing from Bēltani. Perhaps she was only abusive towards those who showed vulnerability. Yet Iltani was not getting any closer to becoming a scribe. She read and reread all the tablets she had made under Amat-mamu's tutelage in order not to forget what she had learned. She knew the signs by heart, and how to press the reed-stylus in the damp clay.

However, she discovered that the bathhouse was a good place to get to know the other *nadītu,* so she began to go there more often. Still she had not found a good friend. She took up weaving, an occupation many *nadītu* enjoyed. She was not very good in it, nor did she really enjoy it much.

Time passed slowly, and Iltani found herself occasionally giving way to self-pity again. A year from now, at the latest, she consoled herself, she would be free to find a tutor outside the *gagû.* She would just have to be patient.

Every night she prayed to the gods, asking them not to forget her, to send her help.

* * *

One late afternoon, on her way home from the bathhouse, Iltani saw Parratum waving excitedly.

"Mistress Iltani, come quickly," called Parratum, "you need to see this."

Iltani hurried home. Covering nearly the whole length of her room were baskets of clay tablets, hundreds of them in various sizes.

"Did you know about this, Mistress?" Parratum asked. "The baskets were delivered by the servants of Reš-Aja. Do you know her?"

"The name sounds familiar," said Iltani, but she could not remember where she had heard it.

"Is it a gift?" asked Parratum.

"I have no idea." Iltani was utterly perplexed.

"Well, I must go and prepare the dinner," she said, leaving Iltani to enjoy the treasure she found.

Iltani picked up a tablet at random from one of the baskets. It looked like a contract. She went over to another basket and looked through the texts. They were lexical lists.

Spellbound, she sat down on her mattress. Was this really happening?

And then, she jumped up and covered her mouth with both hands so that her shout of exultation would not be heard. "Thank you Šamaš, Aja and Nabû, for this mysterious gift!" It was the sign she had prayed for.

There were countless signs she did not recognize, but she was not discouraged. On the contrary, here was a challenge she would gladly take up. Iltani perused the tablets until it was too dark to see anything even by the light of the oil lamps. Parratum's cooked meal was left untouched. Iltani was in ecstasy, and food was the last thing on her mind.

* * *

A few days later, as she sat absorbed in the tablets, Iltani was startled by a voice behind her.

"I am Reš-Aja. We met at your initiation to the *gagû*, though I do not really expect you to remember." Her smile was genuine; she projected warmth and kindness. Iltani stood up, facing her surprise guest. "It was you who led me to the room where I was anointed," Iltani said, vaguely recalling the ceremony.

"I was sad to hear about your losses, your aunt, Amat-Šamaš, and your friend. I also heard that you are on your way to becoming a scribe."

"Well, perhaps," Iltani said timidly.

Reš-Aja picked up one of the tablets and ran her hand over it. "You must be wondering why I am here. You see, I cannot read or write, but I run a thriving business that often requires me to deal with records and letters and such. And so, in brief, I would like you to become my personal scribe."

Iltani listened closely. "But I have not finished my studies. I am not even through with the basics yet."

"Have you not learned enough with your teacher already to continue learning on your own?" Reš-Aja asked encouragingly. I believe these tablets I sent over may help you get started."

109

Iltani contemplated the words of her guest. Who was she? Another bird of prey like Bēltani? No. Iltani did not sense that. This woman seemed genuinely eager to help her. Was she right? Could she continue learning on her own?

"Yes, these tablets may be a good way to start though I fear it may take some time for me to fully master the art of the scribe," Iltani finally said.

"I have time. Start learning. If you have any problems, come to me."

Iltani's heart overflowed with gratitude to the gods and to this stranger, her benefactor. She bowed. "Thank you, Reš-Aja. I will work very hard. I am indebted to you for the tablets. How can I repay you? With silver?"

"To have you for my personal scribe will be ample pay. But there is a favor I would like to ask of you, one that need not be postponed until you are a full-fledged scribe."

Iltani missed a heartbeat. So there was a price for these tablets.

"I would like to introduce you to Awat-Aja, a *nadītu* who entered the *gagû* around the same time as you. She has not found many friends here. I would like you to help her."

"But how?"

"You will find the right way, I am certain."

* * *

Over the following days Iltani could scarcely tear herself away from the tablets. She decided that the best way to proceed was to sort them according to categories: lexical lists, letters, poetry, contracts, arithmetic tables and omens based on the entrails of sacrificial animals.

* * *

Every morning, on her return from temple prayers, after she had eaten her morning meal and offered food and water to Amat-Šamaš's votive statue, Iltani set to work on the lexical lists. She decided to learn ten to twenty new signs a week, memorizing and copying them the way Amat-Mamu had shown her.

Then she would try to read a document: a letter, a contract, a poem. When she came across a sign she did not know, she listed it on a moist clay tablet she could add to every day.

Later, in the early afternoon, she would study arithmetic, or read omen-tablets.

One morning, as she was absorbed in copying signs with her stylus, she thought she recognized a certain tablet. Where had she seen it before? Had she read it with Amat-Mamu? Impossible. Surely she was mistaken.

"Reš-Aja is here to see you, Mistress," Parratum said, interrupting her.

Reš-Aja entered with a smile. "I would like to invite you to dine with me and Awat-Aja. I think you deserve a break from all this learning," she said.

"Reš-Aja." Iltani greeted her benefactor, looking into her eyes. "You are indeed a messenger of the gods. These tablets, these precious gifts, have given meaning to my days. I offer you thanks with all my heart," she said, and bowed her head in reverence.

"I appreciate your hard work, Iltani. And you can express your gratitude by dining with me and Awat-Aja."

* * *

When they arrived at Reš-Aja's house Iltani saw Awat-Aja and remembered her. She was the girl who had looked so angry the night of the initiation. She still had a sullen look about her.

"This is Awat-Aja," Reš-Aja said, "and this is Iltani." She turned to Awat-Aja. "You may find each other's company helpful, perhaps even interesting."

Iltani liked Awat-Aja right away. There was something feisty about her, full of spirit. Her dark green eyes matched her sharp way of speaking. Reš-Aja asked them about their families, and while Iltani elaborated with amusing stories and descriptions of Sin-rēmēni, Awat-Aja kept her answers short. After the meal, Reš-Aja insisted that they meet again soon, without her this time, and they both agreed. Iltani planned to help Awat-Aja shed her resentments so she would never become a *nadītu* of the desperate kind. The two of them would be friends, she decided.

Chapter 12

"To think, you come from Babylon, the royal city. What is it like?" Iltani asked wide-eyed the first time Awat-Aja came to visit.

"When you enter the gates, you are in a different world: garden terraces and towers and ferry-boats on the river. I miss my beautiful home."

"What about your family; what is your father's profession? Do you have siblings?"

"*Abu* is a merchant. He trades in timber from the land of the cedars and in precious stones. I have two older brothers," she added, her voice full with contempt.

"Were you unhappy at home?"

"No, I loved my life back then," Awat-Aja added quietly, pressing her lips hard against each other. "Before I came here I was engaged. I was about to get married."

"What happened? How is it that you became a *nadītu*?" Iltani asked hesitantly. She saw Awat-Aja's painful expression.

Awat-Aja pursed her lips, then she spoke quietly. "There was a young man, very pleasing in looks and manner, who asked to marry me. The engagement was about to be arranged. But one day he stopped appearing in our courtyard. My brothers were strangely silent about it, but I believe they were to blame."

"Why? What did they do?" Iltani asked, aghast.

"*Abu* is old, you see, and my brothers manage our lands. *Abu* was going to give me a generous dowry including some of the larger properties. That would have sorely diminished my brothers' inheritance. I think they may have paid my suitor to go away, or perhaps they even threatened him. Then they persuaded *Abu* that since there were no other suitors in sight, for the sake of family honor, I should become a *nadītu*. I fought and pleaded with *Abu*, but he sided with my brothers, wishing to see his dear little daughter safe behind a wall." Awat-Aja sneered. "The *gagû* of Sippar has the most prestige, so here I am," she added sadly.

"Yes it was, very painful. It is still painful," Awat-Aja whispered, and looked at her new friend, wondering whether to say more, or leave it at that. Finally she smiled, though her eyes stayed sad. "Our home is near the palace, the E-sagila and not far from the *kārum* and the river gate. We have two courtyards, a large one where the merchants and traders meet with *Abu* and a smaller courtyard in the back, just for the family, next to the two sleeping rooms. When I was little, I would hide there from my brothers and they could never find me!" She gazed in the air, lost in reverie.

"I used to love going to the *kārum* with *Ummu* to shop for wares, and to try on different kinds of the richest cloth, even cloth from the land of the Nile. I never came home empty-handed. I was one of the best dressed girls in Babylon. *Ummu* saw to that," she sighed. "I miss seeing the palace in all its splendor, gold and blue and green, inscriptions everywhere. You would certainly enjoy reading those." Awat-Aja looked sadly at Iltani.

There was so much longing in her eyes. Iltani had come to realize how many girls despised the *gagû* and bemoaned their destiny. Perhaps she could do something to cheer her new friend.

"Would you like me to teach you how to read and write? I mean, I am still learning myself, but it might be enjoyable to learn together," said Iltani.

"I, learn to read?" Awat-Aja said. "What for?"

"For no particular reason; just for the joy of it."

"The joy of it?" Awat-Aja responded in disbelief. "Joy is preparing for a wedding. Joy is dressing in the finest cotton gowns."

"Well, I believe that learning is a joy. Come, let's give it a try. What can it hurt? At least you will be well-occupied."

Awat-Aja reflected a moment. "All right, we could try. It may turn out that learning the art of the scribe is a sheer pleasure," she said, teasing her new friend.

Iltani knew she was on the right path. Though not yet a full-fledged scribe she had acquired her first pupil. In time, both *nadītu* gained a great deal more than just becoming a teacher and pupil, they found a friendship that would last for many years.

* * *

Iltani spent most of her days copying tablets and memorizing signs. Before long, she was able to write letters for Reš-Aja and serve as her scribe. However, she found that teaching was even better than learning. Iltani put much thought into making the lessons interesting and not too repetitive.

Awat-Aja was a diligent student and Iltani enjoyed her company. She felt less alone when they spent time together and Awat-Aja seemed less sullen now that her days were filled with learning and also a new activity, weaving and dying cloth, the finest in the *gagû*. It wasn't long before she was the best-dressed *nadītu* in Sippar.

* * *

"I have a present for you," Reš-Aja announced.

"By Šamaš and Aja. You have already given me so much," Iltani said.

"Well, this is a tool every scribe needs. You can use it to seal letters or when you are called upon to serve as a witness. Here open it," she said, handing Iltani a small leather pouch.

Iltani pulled the string and spilled the contents out into her hand. It was a beautiful lapis lazuli cylinder-seal with an inscription and an image of a man standing before the god Šamaš. The seal was strung on a sturdy cord.

"Thank you," Iltani muttered in astonishment. The seal was beautiful indeed but what excited her most were the words inscribed upon it: Iltani MUNUS.DUB.SAR: Iltani, the female scribe.

"It is a great happiness for me to have seen you overcome the obstacles that stood in your way," Reš-Aja said, and hugged Iltani.

"May Šamaš and Aja and Nabû keep you healthy forever," Iltani said, blessing her, overjoyed with the gift.

* * *

Life took its course. The pain of the first few months dimmed to a vague memory and Iltani arrived at the conclusion that she had been tested, not punished by the god Nabû. He wanted to make sure she was steadfast in her desire to become a scribe, and as a reward, he had sent Reš-Aja and the tablets to her. Iltani was determined to become the best female-scribe in the *gagû* and a teacher of other *nadītu*. Iltani's second Nissanu approached and with it, the New Year's festival, the *Akitu*. She had missed the first one while taking care of Amat-Šamaš.

"You must come, you must!" insisted Awat-Aja. "To be invited to celebrate the *Akitu* at the Princess's house is a great honor. Not everyone is invited."

"I am not especially fond of *gagû* gatherings," said Iltani, searching for a good excuse not to go as she was sure Bēltani would be there.

"It was Reš-Aja who arranged for us to be invited, and you would not want to upset her, would you?" asked Awat-Aja.

"Of course not," Iltani said crossly. "All right, then, I will go."

"Thanks to the gods!" Awat-Aja exclaimed. "And for once, my dear friend, you will not wear some color-undefined, with clay-stained rag."

"So that's why you are so eager for me to go," Iltani said, smiling at Awat-Aja, the flower of the *gagû*, who would only consent to wear a simple dress for the weekly scribal lesson.

"I trust you will make me look at least as good as the Princess."

"That will be no easy matter with those mud-colored hands of yours," Awat-Aja said laughing. "How will we ever wash them clean?"

Iltani looked down at her hands with satisfaction, hands that could write almost as fast as a person could speak, the supple hands of a scribe.

"I love them, stained though they may be. . ."

"Yes, yes. We know. Your pretty bear-paws," Awat-Aja interrupted. "Now listen, I will dress you like a princess for the *Akitu* only you must promise to keep the 'pretty bear-paws' out of sight."

They burst out laughing.

* * *

"I bid you welcome and thank you for celebrating the *Akitu* with me," said the Princess on her throne. Her long, dark-brown hair was gathered in the back. She wore a gown with golden stripes that reflected the torchlight in the courtyard, shimmering golden bangles on her arms and a large gold ring embedded with lapis lazuli. She looked majestic, more like a queen than a princess, thought Iltani.

Once the guests were seated, the music began; lyres and flutes, bells and drums. Singers trilled songs of the creation and the dancers whirled. The sumptuous food and drink reminded Iltani of her initiation feast: crisp, grilled fish, soup and breads of many kinds served with date honey and sesame oil, and after that, sweet cakes with fresh and dried fruits and a special liquor.

"There is so much food!" said Iltani.

"Yes, and at the end of the feast each guest receives a basket of food to take home with a small surprise inside," Awat-Aja informed her.

"How do you know that?"

"Reš-Aja told me."

Iltani observed the crowd and her eye fell on Amat-Mamu. She was looking straight at her. They were locked in a stare. And then Amat-Mamu raised the corners of her mouth in a tiny smile. Only someone who knew her well would have recognized it as such. Yet there it was. Iltani was confused. Why would Amat-Mamu smile at her? She was sure Bēltani must be close by, but as she carefully released herself from Amat-Mamu's gaze and searched for Bēltani in the crowd she could not find her. There were about forty *nadītu* present and Bēltani was not among them.

"Come Iltani, let me introduce you to the Princess," Reš-Aja tore her away from these thoughts.

"Really?" she said in awe.

Reš-Aja smiled encouragingly.

As they approached the Princess, Iltani saw Amat-Mamu out of the corner of her eye, watching her again, following her movements. It made her anxious. Was Amat-Mamu spying on her, so she could tell Bēltani?

"By Šamaš and Aja, may the gods bless you and keep you healthy forever." Reš-Aja bowed to the Princess and Iltani did the same.

"May I introduce you to Iltani, a gifted scribe and a compassionate *nadītu*."

"Draw nearer," the Princess said in a sweet and gentle voice over the music. "I have heard much about your talent. You know, I have an extraordinarily large library here and I should be pleased to put it at your disposal. You may come and use it any time you like. My scribes will be glad to assist you."

Iltani was overjoyed. She bowed and thanked the Princess.

"I hope you enjoy the rest of the *Akitu* celebration," said the Princess.

* * *

Towards the end of the feast, Iltani saw Amat-Mamu coming straight toward her. In a panic, she searched for Awat-Aja, but she was on the far side of the courtyard. Iltani stood up.

"I was happy to hear that you are becoming quite a good scribe," Amat-Mamu said. "And as your former teacher I am proud." Her words surprised Iltani, and just at that moment, she remembered the tablet Reš-Aja had sent to her among the others, the one she had seen before but could not place. It was Amat-Mamu's, she was sure now. She had read it once in her library.

"Thank you," Iltani answered in confusion. "You gave me a good foundation so I could continue on my own."

"I wish you well," she said and turned abruptly.

Iltani stood there, stunned. Was it Amat-Mamu who had arranged for the tablets to be brought to her house? Then how and why was Reš-Aja involved?

Perhaps Amat-Mamu had wanted her to become a scribe? Iltani thought. She searched the crowd for Amat-Mamu, but she had gone. Iltani knew that was another secret she would have to keep, for her former teacher's sake. In that moment, Iltani understood that those who have an opportunity to help have an obligation to do so, even at personal risk. Amat-Mamu had taken a risk to help her become a scribe. And she, Iltani, will have to do all in her power to make sure Bēltani won't harass another *nadītu*. She went to the Princess and respectfully asked her for an audience, which she was granted. She was to come in a few days to the Princess.

Even if I have to reveal what has happened to me, I will make sure Bēltani will think twice before trying to bother another woman, Iltani thought as she returned home, looking forward to her future meeting with the Princess.

* * *

"Wear it on your wrist and think of it as a piece of jewelry, which it actually is. An amulet to keep you safe outside the *gagû* walls," Reš-Aja explained to Iltani. "Long ago the *nadītu* were not allowed to leave under any circumstances. The rule was changed by Hammurabi's grandfather. Now that you have been here two years, you have earned a little freedom," Reš-Aja declared.

"I feel strange about seeing my family. I have not visited them since the funeral," Iltani said.

"That is understandable. But remember, you are more seasoned now than you were a year ago. You are a scribe, you have friends, and well. . ." Reš-Aja looked at her tenderly. "I am not your real family, but I consider you as close as a child of my own would be."

"Thank you, Reš-Aja," Iltani said sincerely. She had felt happier, she admitted, since Reš-Aja's appearance in her life.

"Now, my dear, enjoy the visit. Your *Abu* and *Ummu* will be very proud of you indeed."

* * *

Seeing Iltani walking away, happy and content, Reš-Aja remembered a conversation she had a few months earlier.

"I require your help, Reš-Aja," Amat-Mamu had said when they met in the foul-smelling tanners' quarter many months earlier. "But I need your assurance that you will tell no one about our agreement. Can I count on you?"

"Of course," Reš-Aja answered.

"Iltani's *Abu* hired me to teach her the scribal arts and I found her to be the best student I ever had," Amat-Mamu had continued. "Her memory is extraordinary; she is a quick study and a hard worker. But for reasons I cannot disclose, I am unable to continue teaching her. It will be a great loss for the *gagû* and for the girl herself if she fails to become a scribe. Especially since I am the only scribe left in the *gagû* now. And I am getting older. This is what I ask of you. Offer Iltani a position as your personal scribe. It must be your idea. She learned the basics from me and she will be able to teach herself now. I will have a cartload of tablets delivered to your house from outside the *gagû*. No one is to know where the tablets came from, that is crucial. You must never reveal my name to anyone. My personal safety depends on your discretion. I am sure that Iltani will be invaluable to you by and by. And for your help to me I am willing to pay you, name your price."

Reš-Aja had been surprised at this offer, but she was well aware that secrets were sometimes a necessity in the *gagû*. She had heard of Amat-Šamaš's unfortunate death, the girl's aunt. Iltani, she realized, was probably lonely and sad without her. And Amat-Mamu was certainly right about the need for another *nadītu* scribe. She happily had agreed to help.

Reš-Aja also remembered how she had another idea, a way to benefit another young *nadītu*. Yes, the two girls would probably get along quite well. They were both a little lonely.

That was many months before. Reš-Aja was happy that she had agreed to help. It turned out beneficial for a few women.

* * *

Iltani approached the gate. Her heart was racing, her stomach turning. Why was she so nervous?

"Iltani," she heard *Abu* call her. "Iltani!" And there was *Ummu* and Sin-rēmēni too. They ran towards her as she walked through the *gagû* gate and embraced her warmly. *Ummu* was in tears, but they were tears of happiness.

"How tall you have grown!" Iltani noted with surprise as she hugged her brother. Sin-rēmēni was ten now, almost as tall as she was.

"Perhaps you shrank," he said, teasing her.

"You are a sight to see, dear daughter," *Abu* said. "Come, let's go home."

"Wait," Iltani stopped them. Could we walk by the river first?" She had been yearning to see the river, to breathe in the tranquility of the flowing water.

* * *

The reunion was a happy one. From now on, Iltani would be free to visit her family more often.

"Tell me about the É-DUBBA, how is it going?" she said to Sin-rēmēni when they went up to the roof.

"Well, actually, not so well. I'm a poor student compared to you and Marduk-ili."

"What do you mean?" Iltani asked.

"It is hard for me to concentrate and remember the signs. I will soon be forced to leave. *Abu* knows."

"Perhaps your teachers are to blame?"

"No, Iltani, I am not clever like you and Marduk-ili. But I think three scribes in one family are quite enough, don't you?" His laugh was genuine.

"What does *Abu* say?"

"He is more understanding than *Ummu*."

Iltani smiled warmly and gazed into his eyes. "The important thing is to find the path of fortune ordained for you by the gods, and you will, little brother, I am certain of it."

* * *

The day flew by as Iltani regaled her family with stories about the *gagû* and her new friend and her work as Reš-Aja's scribe. They planned another family visit soon, a feast next time. Sin-rēmēni went off with Humbaba, now full grown though he still was playful like a puppy. Iltani was glad for *Abu*'s company on the way back to the *gagû*. She sensed he had something important to say.

"I cannot tell you how distressed I was to hear from Amat-Mamu that she planned to stop your lessons. I offered to pay her more money, but she refused without explanation."

"It does not matter anymore, *Abu*," Iltani said reassuringly. "Sometimes the gods lead us in unexpected directions. But you see, I am a scribe now, just as we always planned. I am happy." She told him animatedly about her new tablet collection and the Princess's invitation to use her library and about her new friend who had become her first pupil and the joy she found in teaching. She spoke only about her happy experiences. She would not tell *Abu* the truth about Amat-Mamu and Bēltani. She was a grown woman now. She would deal with it herself.

They parted at the *gagû* gate. No tears. No sadness, just a long, warm embrace.

"I will be home again soon for the feast, *Abu*," Iltani promised.

"May Šamaš, Aja and Nabû keep you safe and healthy," *Abu* said, blessing her, kissing her forehead.

Passing through the gate, Iltani felt as though a great burden had been lifted from her shoulders. She was a scribe now, refining her skills. She had a friend and protector in Reš-Aja. Her meeting with the Princess had gone very well. The Princess was shocked to hear of Bēltani's conduct and promised to warn her severely. Iltani did not fear her anymore. The crisis had made her stronger for whatever lay ahead. Her family was well, and she would be able to visit them from time to time now. She thanked the gods for her good fortune and prayed that they would protect her loved ones.

With those pleasing thoughts she reached home, happy in the anticipation of her continued life as a *nadītu* and a scribe.

Chapter 13

"YOU FELT VERY CLOSE TO HER, didn't you?" Awat-Aja asked as she hugged Iltani and tried to comfort her.

"Kunutum was my aunt's best friend. She looked after me when I had no one else in the *gagû*. If not for her I might have starved to death in my room," Iltani said.

Iltani and Awat-Aja joined the funeral procession of *nadītu* and wailing women. At the cemetery, Iltani placed bread and a small vessel filled with oil in the pit for Kunutum to take to the world of the dead.

On their way home, she and Awat-Aja took a walk along the river. Sitting down under a date palm on the bank, watching the slow green-brown waters of late summer flow by, Awat-Aja reflected: "Nine years since we entered the *gagû*. I can hardly believe it, can you?"

"No. Not really," Iltani said, gazing at the water, her hair fluttered by a light breeze. "The gods have blessed us." She expressed her thankfulness aloud.

I suppose I am happy, too," said Awat-Aja. "I have accepted the life of the *gagû*, and my fabric industry is thriving as I never thought possible. It is certainly useful to know how to read. And I have also lived up to my mother's expectations. I am the best dressed *nadītu* in all of Sippar," Awat-Aja joked without bitterness. She took Iltani's hand. "Come, let us go home."

* * *

"How should I start this time?" Iltani wondered aloud as she paced the courtyard, inspecting every object that met her eyes as though she expected to find the answer there.

Two new pupils were about to arrive. Her gaze fell on a pile of pottery shards. "Of course," she exhaled, and entered her workroom.

By now she had trained many *nadītu* in the scribal arts but last year's pupils had not shown much zeal. It was tedious, trying to pass knowledge on to girls who only wanted to learn the rudiments and had no real interest in becoming scribes.

They came because their families had signed a contract with her for a stipulated number of lessons and the money she was to be paid.

Parratum walked out to the courtyard. "The two new girls are waiting by the door, Mistress," she said.

"Show them in. And please bring us the water jug and three cups."

Iltani went back to her room and the two young *nadītu* walked in. The tall one wore a bright dress with bold red stripes and the other, shorter and slightly plump, wore a darker gown of red, brown and ochre wool. Lovely cloth, Iltani noted, Awat-Aja's, possibly.

She had thought of a way to encourage the young *nadītu* from the outset without making them feel like children and she hoped it would work: to begin with the material itself.

"Good morning, young ladies," she said, greeting them warmly. "As you have probably been told, my name is Iltani. Let me assure you that the art of reading and writing looks harder than it really is. But, before we start our lesson today, I would like for you to become familiar with the materials of the scribe."

Iltani approached the chest in the corner of the room and opened it. "Now, please, each of you, take a piece of clay."

The shorter *nadītu* walked up and chose a small chunk of clay wrapped in damp cloth. She began to knead it. The other girl, Lamassani, stayed put. "Why should I get my hands dirty? I don't know how to read or write and I have no interest in learning," she snapped at Iltani.

Iltani had not anticipated such a response. This was no way to address a teacher. The girl was impudent, to say the least. Yet something about her manner, something in her tone of voice betokened that the outburst had not been directed personally against her. Iltani recognized the anger; she had seen it in Awat-Aja and other young *nadītu*. She decided to scold her, but just enough to set down the rules.

"Lamassani," Iltani said as sternly as she could," in this room you will do as I tell you, even when you see no reason to. Furthermore," she added, carefully choosing her words, "I ask that you speak to me as you would have others speak to you."

Lamassani waited a moment, then nodded and walked over to the chest. She chose a rather large chunk of clay.

"Now, let us smell the clay. Does it remind you of anything? Can you describe the smell?"

The two *nadītu* sniffed the clay and giggled.

"It smells like mud, like mud near the river."

"I disagree," said Lamassani sarcastically. "It smells exactly like my mother's cooking!" The other *nadītu* gasped, half in laughter, half in shock.

"Yes, and other than that, is there anything you would like to add?" Iltani asked, mildly amused. This girl had a razor sharp tongue.

Lamassani stared through Iltani at a non-existent point in the air, contemplating what to do. It was not the teacher's fault she was there. Her parents had forced her to enter the *gagû*. They had paid for these lessons. And maybe something useful would come of learning how to read and write.

"I smell the dampness of the clay, the moisture in it. I sense how pliable it will be in my hands, how easy to shape," she said, kneading the clay into a little bowl.

"Yes, moisture, the power of water, gives flexibility, the virtue of clay. Keep kneading, get the feel of it. Meanwhile, I'll read you some lines from a story you may have heard."

Iltani went over to the shelf, picked out a large clay tablet, and began to read:

"In those days, the days when heaven and earth were created; in those years, the years when the fates were determined; when the chief gods were born; when the goddesses married and conceived and gave birth; when the younger gods were obliged to toil for their board, for their bread; the greater gods oversaw the work, and the younger gods endured it. They dug canals and they began to complain about this life."

"So you see, the younger gods had to serve the older ones, cooking for them, building, cleaning, digging canals, and they complained about their lot, and that is why Enki— creator of all the gods—and his consort Ninmah took a piece of clay and fashioned the first human beings and planted them in the wombs of two goddesses. The children born from the wombs of these goddesses were the ancestors of all people on earth. People were created to serve the gods."

"I know that story. But what does it have to do with reading and writing?" Lamassani asked defiantly.

"The clay you hold in your hands is the same clay, the raw material Enki used to form the first human beings. And like a human being, everything we write on clay has a life of its own. For example, a person writes a letter to a friend, the friend answers, other consequences follow. And if we copy a story on a clay tablet, the story may be read long after we are gone. The words on the clay live forever. Clay with writing comes to life, just as clay shaped by the gods produced human beings."

"But if you do not burn the tablet, if you soak it in water, it will turn back to clay again," remarked the shorter *nadītu*.

"Yes, that is true. But even then, the tablets have a life. They can be used over and over again, with new inscriptions each time. So, you may think that what you're holding in your hands is only a lump of clay, but this same clay with writing on it will be a new creation with a life of its own, and who can tell where it will lead?"

"Well I can tell where my life is leading," Lamassani remarked in deep despair. "The *gagû* and nowhere but the *gagû*!"

Iltani looked in her eyes with concern. She remembered Tabbija's and Awat-Aja's utter hopelessness. What could she say to Lamassani? That the agony would pass? No, any answer she gave the girl now would be the wrong answer. There was nothing she could say in solace.

"I don't know, Lamassani," Iltani said to her in a compassionate voice, "perhaps if you turn in prayer to Šamaš and Aja, they will ease your sorrow, and. . ." she smiled at her, "working with clay is also good. It may give you a purpose." Whether or not her words made any sense to Lamassani, she could not tell, but she hoped they would. Behind all the anger and aggression, she sensed a strong-minded, intelligent girl.

Iltani gave both pupils some damp cloth to cover the clay. Their assignment was to knead it and shape it into a tablet before their next lesson.

After they left, as she sat in her room reading, Iltani heard a sound of drumming and commotion. She went out to the courtyard and listened. No, these were not the usual sounds for this time of day. The beating drums and the rumbling of horse-drawn chariots grew louder, and seemed to advance in the direction of the Šamaš temple.

Iltani told Parratum she was going out to see what the uproar was about. Surely the gatekeeper will know, she thought as she headed for the *gagû* gate. Through the open gates, she could see a large crowd carrying baskets.

"What is going on? What are all these people doing here?" she asked the gatekeeper.

"Have you not heard? King Hammurabi is on his way to visit the Princess at the Šamaš-temple, and he is bringing gifts to the temple. They say the King will present the temple with a huge stone today." A few more *nadītu* huddled at the gate to watch.

Iltani was curious, eager to catch sight of the King. She had seen him only once before, and from some distance. "Let's go watch," she said to the other *nadītu* standing nearby.

"No, it is too crowded out there for me. And too many horses," answered one of the *nadītu*.

"I doubt we will be able to get more than a glimpse of him," added another. "And anyhow, he will probably ride directly into the High Priest's courtyard where they will never let us in!"

But Iltani was not about to miss such an opportunity. The High Priest's courtyard, with its emblem of Šamaš, was open in for offerings twice a day for everyone, and also a special time for the *nadītu* in the morning and afternoon. Being a scribe, however, Iltani had been there many times when it was closed to the public, witnessing documents that had to be sworn before the emblem of Šamaš.

Iltani hurried back inside the *gagû* and ran straight to the chief-scribe's workroom next to the UGULA's chamber.

* * *

Iltani entered just as the chief-scribe was on his way out. He and Iltani were not the best of friends. Though he would never admit it, he was jealous of her. Both knew that she was the more able scribe. Still, he tried to be fair and often asked Iltani for her services, especially since she was the best female scribe in the *gagû*.

"Please, come with me to see the King in the High-Priest's courtyard," she asked breathlessly, knowing that the High-Priest's courtyard was off limits when the King visited Sippar and she would probably not be admitted on her own. After riding through the crowd, the King would no doubt meet with his sister the Princess while he made his offerings to the gods. Only the High Priest and people of exalted station, like the chief-scribe, could enter while the King was there.

"I was just on my way there, come along," he answered with a light smile. Today her scribal gifts would be of no avail to her, he thought smugly to himself.

They walked out together and entered the great courtyard of the temple complex. Hundreds of people stood around, speaking animatedly as they waited for the King to arrive. The chief-scribe and Iltani fought their way through the multitude to the stairway leading to the inner court of the High Priest. Two royal soldiers and one high-ranking priest stood guard at the gate.

"Let me do the talking. I promise you I will get us both in," said the chief-scribe. Iltani, who could be feisty when anyone questioned her authority as a scribe, was quietly deferential today.

The high-ranking priest nodded to the soldiers to let the chief-scribe pass. Just as Iltani was about to go through the gate with him, the priest stopped her: "You may not go in today."

Iltani was about to protest, but the chief-scribe squeezed her hand. "Iltani's services may be needed today, as the personal scribe of the Princess."

It was a white lie. The chief-scribe knew that Iltani had written letters for the Princess on several occasions, but she was not her personal scribe. The high-ranking priest looked puzzled. Why would the Princess need a scribe today, and why couldn't the chief scribe do the writing if necessary? Still, he had too much respect for the chief-scribe to interrogate him at this point, so he let them pass without further ado.

Once inside the inner court, Iltani and the chief-scribe went their separate ways. He joined a group of priests who were talking about the King and his expeditions, and Iltani looked for a good spot to stand and observe.

* * *

Several areas of the court were shaded with date-frond canopies and furnished with carpets and cushions. Iltani positioned herself under one of the canopies, and quietly observed the scene. She recognized a few people: several scribes, a local judge and one of the gatekeepers. She saw the Princess and her servant enter and take their places under a canopy on the other side of the court. Iltani bowed her head respectfully from afar. The Princess smiled and nodded back. Over the years Iltani had met with the Princess several times, discussing matters of the *gagû* and of *nadītu* who may be in need of help. And to the best of her knowledge, after the Princess's intervention with Bēltani, she never bothered a *nadītu* again. Furthermore, the Princess had told her, as a precaution her servants kept an eye on Bēltani's whereabouts and activities.

By now Iltani realized there were other *nadītu* who loved each other in the same manner as men and women did; some of them were her friends. But Bēltani had been different; she had used her powerful position to force herself on others. And then, about two years ago Bēltani had died. Rumors circulated that she had poisoned herself. Whether the rumors were true or false, Iltani did not care. She was happy never to encounter Bēltani again.

The noise behind the doors grew louder, exultant cheers and the neighing and snorting of horses. "May Šamaš keep you in good health forever! May Šamaš and Aja keep you in good health!" roared the crowd.

The doors opened. All faces turned towards the King and his entourage. Iltani was spellbound. She had never

131

seen him at such close range before. He looked so tall and gracious on horseback with his grizzled, tightly curled beard and the golden splendor of his conical crown. He radiated majesty. Just behind him rode another man, considerably younger, perhaps his son, Prince Samsu-iluna, Iltani guessed. But there was something familiar about the younger man. She could not place him, but she knew she had seen him before. She turned her attention back to the King.

The King's servants gripped the horses' reins and the High Priest approached and bowed to the King in greeting: "May Šamaš keep you in good health forever!"

King Hammurabi dismounted and kissed the High Priest on both cheeks.

"I have brought gifts for the glory of Šamaš, god of justice. I am his loyal and humble servant. I am sure you will see to it that my gifts are justly distributed!"

"Thank you, my father," said the High Priest with another deep bow.

Iltani was enthralled, observing the King, his manner, his stature. She peered around and noticed the other rider, who had also dismounted and was staring directly at her. Feeling strange, she looked away. The young man's reddish-curls, his face, where had she seen him before? And why was he staring at her?

When she glanced back in his direction, he was still looking at her, directly into her eyes. Iltani quickly looked down at the mat. She was not used to being stared at in this way.

Her thoughts were interrupted by the exuberant crowd.

"I have brought a special gift to the temple!" the King announced. "Bring in the stone," he commanded his servants. A small wooden wagon was wheeled into the center of the court. On it was an enormous object, covered in cloth. The servants raised the cloth, revealing the corner of a beautiful black diorite stone.

"This black stele will stand in the courtyard engraved with my just verdicts. All who come with offerings to Šamaš, Lord of Justice, will behold it. The gods have willed that I, a pious prince, should reign over the land in righteousness, abolish iniquity and evil so that the strong shall not harm the weak, and establish truth and just laws as the declaration of the land to improve the lot of my people."

Jubilant cheers and blessings filled the court.

From her corner, Iltani could see only a small portion of the stele. She moved in closer, jostling her way through the crowd. The stone was magnificent. It glittered in the sun. What an honor for the temple, she thought.

The crowd pressed forward to behold the beauty of the stele and Iltani drew back to her corner of the vacant canopy. As she observed the people, someone tapped her on the shoulder. When she turned around, her eyes met those of the young man with the reddish curls who had ridden behind the King. Perplexed, she bowed to him. "Prince Samsu-iluna, may Šamaš keep you in good health forever!" she said in awe.

"Me? Prince Samsu-iluna? No, no, I am definitely not the Prince," he said at last, adding with a little laugh. "I am merely one of the King's scribes. But you, Iltani, your fame precedes you, far beyond the gagû. It is said you are better than half the scribes who work for the High Priest."

Iltani was not sure how to react. How did he know her name? Or that she was a scribe?

"Do we know each other?" she finally brought herself to ask.

"I suppose years in the service of the King can change a person." He seemed amused. "You have hardly changed at all. Do you not remember me?"

Iltani's mind raced. This man spoke as if they knew each other yet she had no idea who he was.

"I am Marduk-mušallim. I visited your *Abu*'s house during my last year at the É-DUBBA in Babylon. You were about to enter the *gagû* then, and you asked me questions about the É-DUBBA."

Slowly, vaguely, she remembered him, that shy boy on the roof. But this man, Marduk-mušallim, was grown up and not at all shy.

He was about to say something, when the trumpet blew. The King was ready to leave and Marduk-mušallim had to depart with him.

"I must go with the King, but I am eager to see your work. I am sure we will meet again soon. Very soon," he added, smiling, and without waiting for a reply, hurried back to the King and his attendants.

Iltani did not know what to think of this encounter. She had no idea that people spoke about her scribal work beyond the *gagû*. Occasionally she wrote letters for people outside, but these were usually family friends or acquaintances. And this Marduk-mušallim . . . why did he wish to see her work?

* * *

As the crowd streamed out of the court, Iltani returned home. She still had work to do, in preparation for her next lesson. Over the evening meal, she told Awat-Aja about the King's visit and the gifts he had brought. She began to giggle as she described her mistaking of Marduk-mušallim for Prince Samsu-iluna. Iltani wondered how he recognized her when she hardly remembered him at all.

That night she had a strange dream. In it, she was standing in front of the black diorite stele. She was the chief scribe, and was about to start engraving it when the stone broke into a hundred pieces. In a panic, she hid in the Šamaš-temple and from her hiding place, she could hear Šamaš and Aja discussing their punishment for the chief-scribe who had broken the stone. Šamaš suggested cutting off her hands, while Aja preferred to pluck out her eyes.

134

Iltani woke up in a cold sweat, relieved that it was only a dream.

All the same, the next morning she brought an especially large offering to the temple of Šamaš: a double portion of barley, a costly jug of oil and a tray laden with fruit.

Chapter 14

IN BABYLON, IN THE PALACE LIBRARY of King Hammurabi, five elderly scribes were hard at work formulating the verdicts to be listed on the black diorite stone. They had been engaged in this for months now, surrounded by clay tablets of all sizes covered in wedge-shaped characters. A column of minor scribes arrived bearing yet more tablets. The oldest scribe asked with authority: "Are the opening and ending ready? Where is Marduk-mušallim? Has anyone spoken to him?"

"He has not reported back yet," answered one of the scribes.

"What about the model figure of Šamaš and the King? Is that ready?"

"Yes, that is ready, the sculptor made a few copies," said another scribe.

"All the work must be completed in four weeks' time, do you hear?" said the oldest scribe. "The King wants the work to begin as soon as possible. He has chosen Marduk-mušallim to oversee the engraving. Marduk-mušallim will choose the scribes and he is responsible for the stone. Two of you will accompany him to the Temple of Šamaš in Sippar."

Another elderly scribe frowned with displeasure at the mention of Marduk-mušallim. "The King was mistaken," he muttered under his breath, "to choose so young a scribe, however gifted." The others nodded in agreement.

* * *

The ensuing month was a very busy time for the royal scribes. They had to finish compiling the legal verdicts handed down by the King in the course of his reign. In certain cases, they added other verdicts commonly submitted in the courts. They worked all day, sometimes late into the night by the light of oil lamps. The younger scribes ran tirelessly back and forth bringing more tablets, baskets of food and drink and oil to keep the lamps burning.

By the end of the month, the work was completed; the final drafts of the tablets were wrapped in wool and packed in large, straw-padded hampers. Marduk-mušallim oversaw everything. The hampers were loaded onto three donkey-drawn wagons.

Just before the royal caravan set off to Sippar, the King summoned Marduk-mušallim to the throne room.

"As I am not young anymore; this may be my last great accomplishment," said the King. "I know I have charged you with a most arduous task. I have full confidence in you, Marduk-mušallim. You have grown close to my heart and you will play a part in the future of my son, my heir. This is your final test."

Marduk-mušallim felt great admiration towards the King, he was thunderstruck by his words. He knew the King liked him and respected his work, even though he was much younger than the other scribes in high positions. But to hear these words from the King himself was a great honor.

"I am overcome with gratitude that you have chosen me, my King, my father," he said, bowing. "I hope I will not disappoint you. Thank you for the confidence you have placed in me. May Marduk bless you and keep you healthy forever."

* * *

Marduk-mušallim, his personal servant, and the other scribes gathered around the wagons. A large troop of

Hammurabi's soldiers stood by to accompany the convoy to Sippar, which was situated about forty kilometers north of Babylon. On horseback, without baggage, a person could travel the road in less than a day. But this was a convoy, with clay tablets that had to be handled with care. The servants packed all the necessary provisions to camp out overnight and loaded them on the wagons. Then they climbed up themselves, joined by the two scribes. Marduk-mušallim mounted his horse and led the convoy off.

It was late in the morning next day when the convoy arrived in Sippar. Excitement filled the streets. Once inside the city walls, they were accompanied by curious children running next to the royal carts and adults watching with much interest.

The High Priest greeted them at the temple gate. "May Šamaš and Marduk bless you. The servants are waiting to carry the tablets to the inner court. We have prepared a meal for you and your servants; you must be hungry and thirsty from the journey."

"I thank you for your kindness. May the gods bless you," Marduk-mušallim replied.

Marduk-mušallim was given a room for his stay near the High Priest's chamber in the inner courtyard, away from the day-to-day activities of priests and worshipers. The copy tablets were stored in his room for safekeeping, and the stele was set up in the inner court and covered with woolen blankets.

After the meal, Marduk-mušallim withdrew to his room. He wanted to reflect—he had a certain idea.

* * *

"Here, this should be high enough," said the sculptor in charge of the bas relief depicting Šamaš and Hammurabi.

"But is it not too high?" Marduk-mušallim asked.

"No, any lower and there will not be enough space for the text," said the other scribe.

"Fine, mark the line with chalk and start your work. But remember," added Marduk-mušallim, "this is for the King, there is no room for error."

The sculptor chalked a very fine line on the black stone and his work began.

Until the bas relief of Šamaš and Hammurabi was completed, the scribes could only watch. Now Marduk-mušallim was ready to follow up on his idea. He went back to his room and took a piece of clay out of his chest. When he had formed it into a hand-sized tablet, he began to write a message. The sun was still hot so it would not take too long to dry the tablet. He would send the letter in the morning.

* * *

"Mistress Iltani, a temple messenger has delivered this box and a letter for you," Parratum informed her.

"Just leave the letter on the box. I will attend to it after I finish my lesson."

Iltani was not expecting anything. It must be some document from the priests to read or copy, she thought. It can wait. She turned to teach her students.

"Practice a little more next time," Iltani said as she walked her pupil out to the courtyard at the end of the lesson. Let's see what the priests want now, she thought.

She began to read the letter, more astonished with every line. When she finished reading a first time, she reread the letter twice more, making sure she had not misunderstood or mistaken any of the characters. No, she was right. She crouched beside the box and opened it. Inside she found many small rectangular pieces of stone, and at the bottom of the box, tools for engraving them. She picked up a stone; it was so much heavier than clay. She studied its smooth, shiny surface. This stone was well prepared, she mused.

In all her years as a scribe, she had only written on clay with a stylus, though once, some time ago, a scribe who worked for the Princess had allowed her to try engraving on stone with a chisel and hammer. Iltani had hurt her hands so badly, she could barely move them for a week.

She went to her library and brought out a large clay tablet that she set against the wall. Then she chose a smooth stone tablet from the box and took the tools from the box. The first sign was *Šum*, the second *ma*; *Šumma*: if. Two characters should not be too hard, she thought, and began to engrave them very slowly and carefully. She needed more strength for this than she had expected, and the characters came out crooked. She had missed a few times while hitting the chisel, making small cracks into the stone. Working with soft clay was very different. All you had to do was push the reed into the wet clay, in different positions, varying the pressure. If you made a small mistake, it was easy to correct while the clay was wet, or even afterwards. With stone, one mistake and it was all ruined. With that in mind, Iltani worked until her hands were aching. She stopped and looked on the tablet. It was no good, not the quality she was used to producing on clay. Even with practice, she was not sure she would ever reach the necessary level of perfection.

Over the next few days, Iltani canceled all her lessons and persisted in the effort to copy writings from a clay tablet onto stone. Her hands hurt so badly by the end of the day, even Parratum's massage with hot water was of no avail.

* * *

"What are you doing here?" Awat-Aja said with annoyance. "I thought the earth has swallowed you. You missed our bathhouse day, did you forget? You were supposed to come to dinner at my house with Res-Aja. This is not like you." She changed her tone and asked with concern. "Is everything all right?"

"I am so sorry, I forgot." Iltani weighed her words. "I was working on something new. Everything else slipped from my mind."

"I see," Awat-Aja replied, sounding relieved and irritated at the same time. "I am glad you are not sick. Whatever is so important, you have to take a break from it. I need your help. I am having legal problems with my brothers again. Since *Abu* died they have been ignoring my existence. They have even stopped providing me with barley, oil and cloth. I still have enough from my business, but they cannot treat me this way. I went to the judge in the courtyard of the Šamaš temple and asked him about the law, and I complained to my family, but nothing happened. I want you to write a letter to someone I know, a family friend in a high position. I need the letter to be of the best quality, so I prefer you write it," she said. "After that, I want to hear what you have been working on so hard that you forgot me," she added, her voice still tense.

"All right," Iltani pushed everything aside. "I am sorry to hear about your troubles. Let me get some clay and we will write the letter."

When Iltani came back with a new tablet for the letter, her friend shrieked out loud. She had only then noticed Iltani's hands.

"By Šamaš! What have you done to your hands?"

Iltani's hands were covered with cuts, bruises and scabs peeling off in several places. One finger was dark blue, almost black, and the little finger of her left hand was wrapped in a red-stained plaster bandage.

"It is not as bad as it looks. But I may be left with a shortened finger, and I think I lost the nail too," said Iltani, oblivious to Awat-Aja's shock, or the pain the work caused her. "It is so much harder to work with a chisel engraving on stone than with clay."

"Did you ask the *asû* to treat your wounds? And why are you working on stone anyway?" Awat-Aja asked, shuddering at the sight of Iltani's bandaged finger.

"I will tell you after we write your letter. Come let's begin."

Awat-Aja was at a loss for words. Never had she seen such battered hands. Slowly she began to dictate what she wished to say, and Iltani, effortlessly it seemed, and uncomplaining, wrote down her words.

"To Gimilia say, thus says Awat-Aja. May Šamaš and Aja keep you healthy. What I am entitled to it is written in my tablet of inheritance. Until now, the tablet was deposited with my lady, and so I had not read it. That is why I have not taken legal action against my brothers yet. But since my father died, my brothers have withheld the dowry that is accorded to me in my tablet. Today the meaning of the law was made clear to me, 'a nadītu whose brothers, in her difficulties, do not provide for her, may give her inheritance to whomever she wishes.' I will turn to the judges for help. Send me your final decision on the matter. I shall dispatch my servant and ask that you to send back with her the provisions of food, clothing, oil, and offerings that are due me. Do not waste my dowry!"

After she had finished writing the long letter and put it out in the sun to dry, Iltani told Awat-Aja all that had happened over the past week.

"You mean he invited you to join the scribes who will engrave King Hammurabi's stone? What an honor! But isn't the condition of your hands and especially one finger which will be shorter forever not a very high price to pay?"

"First I must prove that I can write on stone as well as I write on clay. That is what I have been working on so hard, practicing for hours on end. My hands will heal, do not worry. Except for my little finger, though. I fear I will be left with only nine nails." Iltani smiled proudly.

"I cannot understand you," Awat-Aja said, shaking her head.

"For a scribe to join in such a worthy enterprise, for a female scribe even to be asked to join is so great an honor, it is worth the loss of a little skin. Today I finished practicing on the last stone, and I think it is acceptable."

"Let us hope so, otherwise I might find you with only eight fingers left next time," Awat-Aja quipped. "Promise me you will take care. Honor or no honor, I want my best friend whole, with ten fingers and all."

"Never fear!" Iltani laughed.

* * *

After Awat-Aja left, Iltani picked up the last stone and the clay tablet and called Parratum.

"Listen, I must go to the temple now. When my students arrive, tell them to start copying the tablet I have left on the table; they will see it."

She put the stone in a basket and hurried to the High Priest's court. She told the gatekeeper she had come to see Marduk-mušallim, hiding her hands as best she could.

"I will look for him, wait here," he ordered and left the gate to another guard.

He soon returned with a servant. "You may go in, he will see you now. The servant will help you with the basket." Iltani gladly agreed.

* * *

The first thing that caught her eye was Marduk-mušallim's back and his bouncing red curls as he kneeled on the floor, swinging a hammer on the chisel, engraving a stone-table.

Iltani greeted him as she walked around to face him. "May Šamaš keep you healthy."

Marduk-mušallim put down the tools and wiped his forehead. He smiled to his guest.

"May Šamaš and Aja keep you healthy, Iltani. I am very glad to see you have decided to take up the challenge." He stood up. "Let me see your work." He dismissed the servant. "Thank you, you may leave us now."

Iltani gazed curiously around the inner courtyard. The High Priest's inner court was covered with a baked brick floor, surrounded by many rooms. A few canopies roofed with date leaves provided shaded sitting spaces.

"That is the High-priest's chamber, and this one is mine for as long as I am here," Marduk-mušallim said, pointing to his room.

They were alone. The High Priest had probably gone to the temple or to the Ziggurat to attend the gods' needs.

"I brought you the stone I copied, and a clay tablet I wrote," said Iltani as Marduk-mušallim looked into the basket.

Although Iltani had been a scribe for years and knew she wrote better than many of her male colleagues, she was quite jittery. Never before had she been called upon to show her work in this way. She was being tested.

"I must say, I was a little taken aback by your letter," Iltani said.

"Your writing on clay is excellent, the writing on stone is good, but needs more practice," he said, looking the tablets over carefully. "But your reputation does not do you justice; your work is even better than they say."

Iltani felt strange, she had no idea she was known or had a reputation. "Thank you," she said.

Iltani carefully observed Marduk-mušallim. She would never have recognized him. The shy, thin boy she remembered was not at all like the Marduk-mušallim of today, strong, muscular and direct. But his curly red hair was still the same.

"How did you recognize me after all this time?" Iltani asked.

Marduk-mušallim looked up from Iltani's tablets and grinned. "In Babylon there was much talk about a great *nadītu* scribe, and I was curious to meet her. Your name was mentioned, but I did not remember it was you, and of course, Iltani is such a common name. Only when I saw you the day King Hammurabi brought the stone to the temple did I recognize your face, your dimple and remembered our encounter so many years ago. You have not changed much, except for your hands. You had the hands of a young girl then. Now they are the hands of a working scribe."

Iltani put her hands behind her back; she thought he hadn't noticed.

"My hands looked worse when I started practicing on stone. One finger has never healed properly, see?" He showed her a crooked finger, then continued examining her tablets.

"Finished!" Marduk-mušallim said, as he set the clay tablet and the stone on the floor. "I want you to work with me and the other scribes on the stone. I have seen your work, and I count you among the best scribes I have worked with. The King put me in charge of this stone and I have the authority to choose the scribes who will inscribe the stele. There will be four of us, plus the sculptor. The clay tablets were written in Babylon and here we merely copy them to stone." His voice had become serious, commanding.

The moment has come, Iltani thought with a fluttering heart. The invitation was a challenge, but it also filled her with doubt. Was she good enough?

"I am grateful for the trust you place in me," she said.

"We hope to begin the writing a few weeks hence," Marduk-mušallim interrupted her. "The sculptor is carving the figures of Šamaš and Hammurabi now and meanwhile you must work on your engraving with me every day and free yourself of all other obligations," he ordered. "I will choose the part for you to copy and then we will practice together."

Iltani was vexed. She did not like being spoken to in such a way. She was still doubtful. Perhaps it was all a bad idea, and what about her pupils? What of her other work?

"Do you order all your scribes around like this?" she asked boldly. After all, she was not just some scribe; she was a *nadītu* scribe with years of experience.

Marduk-mušallim studied her. Then a smile lit up his eyes and he said: "You have not lost your feistiness."

"Being one of the King's youngest scribes, I have competitors who envy my position and sometimes try to discredit me. I find that showing authority helps."

"All right," Iltani responded, "but I am not one of your scribes, and I am not used to being ordered around. I work for no one but myself." She folded her arms over her chest. "I am still not sure I should take up your challenge, honor though it is. I have pupils and other responsibilities."

"You are right." Marduk-mušallim appeared to regret his stern approach. "You are not below my rank; you are my equal, an excellent scribe, used to working on your own terms, just like me. I would very much like you to take part in inscribing the stele," he said, changing his tone of voice. He had never worked with a woman before, were there other things to consider?

"I have seldom met a scribe as skillful as you, let alone a female scribe, and though I realize that your work must be in high demand, I still cherish the hope that you to will join us in the creation of this once-in-a-king's-lifetime masterpiece," he added with a sheepish smile, his eyebrows arching in anticipation of her reply.

Iltani looked at him and considered her position. She would learn a great deal working with him, engraving on stone. There would never be another opportunity as such. She could handle a little authority.

"I accept. It will be an honor to work with you," she said with a self-command that masked anxiety.

"Excellent," said Marduk-mušallim, breaking into a smile. "I will have more stones brought to you, so you will be able to polish your skills at home. But first, I, no—we— must choose your part of the inscription and practice together. You will have to come here and work with the other scribes. The original clay tablets are not allowed out of the inner court."

Iltani noticed the shift in his intonation. He seemed elated.

"I must go home now. One of my new pupils will be arriving shortly. But as soon as the stones are delivered, I will begin working in earnest."

"Do you have a good plaster for your hands?" Marduk-mušallim asked.

"I do," said Iltani looking down at her hands. "And this is a price worth paying."

* * *

Iltani returned to the *gagû*. She could hardly believe the good fortune that had befallen her. She looked at her hands, forgetting the pain. Her missing fingernail would be her talisman from now on.

Chapter 15

OVER THE NEXT FEW WEEKS, Iltani practiced every day. Apparently being a royal scribe gives one unlimited access to the best materials, she thought, as the next batch of smooth, perfectly processed stones arrived.

She had informed her new pupils that an unexpected development made it necessary to postpone their lessons for the time being. Besides bringing her regular offering to the temple, providing Amat-Šamaš' votive statue with food, and visiting the bathhouse, she neglected everything else, much to Awat-Aja's dismay.

Blisters and bruises of every shape and shade covered Iltani's hands, but the little finger stopped bleeding and she barely noticed the pain, so intense was her pleasure as she saw her mastery increase. At the end of the day, Parratum would soak Iltani's hands in warm water and apply a poultice of sesame and cedar oil, myrtle and myrrh.

Late one afternoon, just as the sun was about to set, a temple servant arrived with a message for Iltani. Marduk-mušallim requested her presence the following morning.

Iltani could hardly sleep, so excited was she. She woke up earlier than usual, and left the house immediately after breakfast.

She entered the temple compound through the connecting gate. It was still too early for daily activities like trials and the examination of witnesses, although devoted worshippers were already bringing their morning offerings to the hall with Šamaš's emblem. Temple scribes wrote out receipts for them and recorded the goods they had brought in their registry. Servants swept the courtyard. Jugs of drinking water were unloaded from a procession of donkeys and transferred to large jars for the public. Iltani passed through the courtyard, greeted an acquaintance and another *nadītu*, and entered the inner court of the High Priest. She was expected, so the guards let her in without delay this time.

The inner court was quiet, and she saw Marduk-mušallim right away.

"May Šamaš and Aja keep you healthy," she said, greeting him.

"I see you have been practicing. Your hands show your hard work." He smiled at her, his face warm and bright.

"Yes, working on stone is quite a challenge," Iltani said.

"Come, let us look at what the sculptor has achieved so far," Marduk-mušallim said.

An enormous cloth draped the lofty stone in the center of the inner court. Marduk-mušallim drew it off.

"It's marvelous." Iltani gasped in wonder. The glossy surface of the stone shimmered in the morning light. She had seen only a section of the stone before, and from a distance. At this close range, it was overwhelmingly impressive, almost alive.

"Here is the winged god Šamaš with his conical crown and his scepter, seated on his throne. You see? And here is Hammurabi, standing before him," Marduk-mušallim explained with pleasure.

"Magnificent!" Iltani was enraptured. "It is so much bigger then I remembered."

"Are you going to start inscribing the laws today?" Iltani asked, hoping to witness the historic event.

"No. I still have some things to prepare first. Would you like to be here when we start? Shall I send for you?" Marduk-mušallim asked.

Iltani sensed an excitement in his voice.

"Yes, I would very much like to watch."

"Very well, then. Now, let us choose the section you will prepare. Is there a type of law that is of particular interest to you?"

Iltani thought about it. She had read and inscribed many trial-records and contracts, and she was familiar by now with the common law concerning *nadītu* from cases she had observed. Perhaps it would be more absorbing to examine laws with which she was unacquainted.

"Well I would like to see what is written about the rights of women in general, and married women in particular."

"Good, they come further on. I will get a few tablets and we will read them together. Then you can decide which ones you would like to work on," he said, and hurried to his room, his reddish curls bouncing with every step. Iltani found this amusing and could not help gazing at his hair whenever he moved.

It took them a long time to read through the many laws. Iltani found all of them interesting. She could not make up her mind which to choose. Finally, she decided on a number of statutes concerning the rights of married or abandoned women.

She read three of the laws out loud:

"If a man should be captured and there are not sufficient provisions in his house, his wife may enter another's house; that woman will not be subject to any penalty.

If a man should be captured and there are not sufficient provisions in his house, and before his return his wife enters another's house and bears children, and afterwards her husband returns to his city, that woman shall return to her first husband; the children shall inherit from their father.

If a man intends to divorce his first-ranking wife who did not bear him children, he shall give back her bride-wealth and restore the dowry she brought from her father's house, and he shall divorce her."

"Perhaps we should set a regular time for our meetings so that you will be able to plan your other activities around them," Marduk-mušallim suggested.

Iltani noticed the difference in his approach. He was not giving her orders anymore; he was cautious in his choice of words. She appreciated his thoughtfulness.

"Yes. How about after the rush of morning offerings?" Iltani proposed.

"That sounds fine. If I find that I am unable to meet with you at that hour, I will send a messenger to inform you in advance."

"My lord, Marduk-mušallim," a servant rushed in. "There is someone looking for you and the gatekeeper will not let him pass. He said it is urgent."

"Iltani," Marduk-mušallim turned to her, "it seems that is all for today. I will see you tomorrow then. My servant will escort you out. I must hurry to see who this is. He may be an envoy from the palace. Would you please cover the stone for me? Thank you, Iltani," he said as he vanished through the small passage.

Iltani approached the stone. The sun, almost at its zenith, gleamed brightly on the stone. The carving at the top was breathtaking. The figures of Šamaš and the King were precisely wrought in every detail, dress, hair, and beard. How elegant they were, compared to the ivory figures on the chest she had received on entering the *gagû*. And this was stone, so much harder to work with than ivory.

"Excuse me, Mistress," the servant said, interrupting her thoughts. "I must get back. May I escort you now?"

"Yes, of course." Iltani quickly draped the cloth over the stone.

* * *

"I am all aflutter. Not since my first lesson with Amat-Mamu have I felt like this," Iltani told Awat-Aja that evening. "Marduk-mušallim has a remarkably agreeable nature. I cannot wait to watch him inscribe the first lines. Tomorrow we will practice together. I imagine he will be a most capable teacher." Iltani fidgeted as she spoke, especially when she went on to describe Marduk-mušallim's bouncing curls.

"Why are you so silent?" Iltani asked her friend. "You have hardly said a word. Are you all right?"

"I am worried about you," Awat-Aja said.

"About me! But why?" Iltani exclaimed.

"I do not want you to get hurt."

"But look, my hands are almost healed. All scribes who work with stone have these scars in the beginning."

"It is not your hands I am worried about, Iltani."

Iltani was perplexed. "What do you mean?" she asked apprehensively.

"He is a man. You are a woman."

"He knows I am a *naditu*. He would never hurt or harm me. We are both well respected scribes and as such we relate to each other," Iltani said with irritation.

"I did not say he would harm you. I merely meant that. . ." Awat-Aja wanted to warn her friend about a feeling, a yearning she would find harder to dismiss as time went by, the torment Awat-Aja had suffered before coming to the *gagû*. But Iltani did not understand. She had never known the affections of a man. Perhaps it really was only about inscribing a stone.

"Of course. You are right." Awat-Aja finished her sentence. "I am happy for you. It is a great honor and a great challenge. Could I come along with you some time and see for myself?"

"Yes! I would love to show you the inscription." Iltani said in excitement. "As soon as there is something to see, I will ask to bring you."

* * *

The following day, Iltani found Marduk-mušallim in the company of two men. He was showing them a specific character and they were discussing the best way to carve it into the stone.

"Iltani." He stopped and greeted her. He introduced the two other scribes, older men whose hair was white.

"May Šamaš and Aja keep you healthy," Iltani said, greeting them.

"May Šamaš keep you healthy too," one of them replied. The other merely nodded into her direction.

"We will continue later." Marduk-mušallim dismissed the scribes, and they left the courtyard. "I will fetch the stones for us to work on," he said to Iltani.

In the meantime, Iltani approached the magnificent black stone. She ran her hand over it, trying to imagine what it would feel like to inscribe it.

"Here," she heard Marduk-mušallim call, and saw the pile of stones he had arranged on a reed mat.

"Today I would like for you to start inscribing a standing stone, which requires a different technique. You have to watch the angles."

Beside the stones lay a clay tablet with one of the texts she had chosen.

"Begin whenever you are ready," he said, smiling encouragingly.

Iltani picked up the chisel and hammer, and regarded the standing stone. She was nervous under Marduk-mušallim's gaze. She placed the chisel on the stone and swung the hammer lightly. A small line appeared on the stone.

"Here, let me adjust your grip and the angle of your arms," said Marduk-mušallim, moving her elbows away from her body. Then he carefully adjusted her right thumb on the hammer. "This will give you more power and better control of it," he said. "Small strokes, don't forget. We have time."

Iltani concentrated, tapping the hammer lightly against the chisel. "Yes it is much better," she said, and looked at the next character on the clay tablet, even though she knew it by heart.

"Wait," Marduk-mušallim said calmly, and she felt his hands moving her elbows away from her body again. This time his grip was stronger, his hands felt warm.

She struck the chisel.

"Much better," Marduk-mušallim said. "You will have no troubles at all."

They practiced for a long while. Marduk-mušallim adjusted Iltani's grip from time to time. Iltani worked quietly, wholly riveted to her task.

"Well done," Marduk-mušallim praised Iltani as he walked her to the temple gate at the end of their session. "I will see you tomorrow."

"Yes, tomorrow," Iltani replied, exhausted but happy.

That night she fell asleep almost before she had undressed.

* * *

In the weeks that followed, they practiced almost daily. Iltani's hands became accustomed to the work. The blue-green bruises faded. They were halfway through the month of Iyyar and the weather was mild, the air sweet and warm with spring. It was a joy to work with Marduk-mušallim; he was knowledgeable and amusing. They often laughed together as they shared their experiences. Iltani told him about her early years in the *gagû*; how she had been forced to learn on her own, though she left out the real reason. She described her pupils and her interactions with the other *nadītu*. Because Marduk-mušallim was a stranger to the *gagû*, she felt perfectly safe talking about the corruption of the UGULA that had presided in her first year in the *gagû*.

Marduk-mušallim told Iltani how he had advanced to the position of the King's scribe, leaving many angry competitors behind. He regaled her with humorous anecdotes about his journeys with the King and his son Prince Samsu-iluna, who would probably succeed him.

Day after day, Iltani watched in awe as Marduk-mušallim inscribed the practice stones with seeming ease. She lost her initial fear and was filled with anticipation. Finally it was time to begin inscribing the beautiful black stele.

* * *

"By Šamaš and Marduk," Marduk-mušallim proclaimed, "the moment has come to carve the first character. I will begin."

"Should we not call the High Priest?" asked one of the other scribes.

"What for?" asked Marduk-mušallim. "Of what help would he be?"

"I don't know, I just thought he should be present for the engraving of the first sign," answered the old scribe with trepidation.

"This moment is sacred only to us, as scribes. No one else could possibly appreciate all the labor we have invested. In time, the King and his people will behold the inscription, but for now, it is for our eyes alone."

Marduk-mušallim set out his special chisel and hammer. "Remember, dear brothers, there is no room for error. Every mistake will endure for eternity. That is what I want you to think about as you work on the stone. You have time, take care—no mistakes."

The sheer excitement of being part of this great enterprise was overwhelming. She watched Marduk-mušallim position himself before the stone. Chisel and hammer in hand, he closed his eyes in silent prayer. Iltani and the other two scribes did not move or breathe. Marduk-mušallim raised his hammer and delivered the first blow. He did not stop, and in a while Iltani made out the words he had inscribed: "*īnu Anum ṣīrum šar Anunakī.* When the august god Anu, King of the Anunnaku deities."

How powerful Marduk-mušallim's hands looked as he worked, yet his movements looked so effortless, he might have been writing on clay.

Would she be as dexterous as he was when her turn came? Suddenly her spirits sank. Perhaps she had been wrong to accept this challenge. What if she made a mistake, or chipped the stone? It will be fine, she told herself, and tried to concentrate on Marduk-mušallim's hands, moving so fluently, creating one character after another to form words and sentences.

"Thank you, Nabû, Šamaš and Marduk," said Marduk-mušallim, laying his tools aside and turning to Iltani and the other scribes. "I will continue to work here, but you are free to go. No need for more than one scribe on the premises now."

"We will leave then," said the older scribes and left.

"I would like to stay a little longer, if I may," said Iltani.

Marduk-mušallim smiled at her. "It would be my pleasure. Please, stay and keep me company. But I must first drink some water." He produced two cups and a small jug of water and poured them both a drink.

Iltani watched him work. Talking to Marduk-mušallim was not like talking to other *nadītu* and scribes, but why, she wondered.

"That is enough for me today," said Marduk-mušallim, wiping his brow.

"How perfect your script is," Iltani said, admiring the stone. "It is so clean and precise. I am afraid I. . ." she paused, her head bowed.

Marduk-mušallim smiled at Iltani. "This is not how I remember our conversation many years ago. As I recall, you nearly bit my head off when I asked why you wanted to become a scribe. Girls can be scribes, too, you said with utmost confidence, and you were certainly right. I chose the very best scribes to work with, and you are one of them. You feel intimidated? Do you think I was not frightened as I struck the first blow just now? My heart was racing and my hands shook. But that is the sign of a good scribe; he who has awe before his work. Especially a stone like this."

Iltani was surprised; he had not seemed nervous in the least to her while working on the stone. But Marduk-mušallim was right, she was indeed terrified of making mistakes, yet she knew she would rise to the challenge.

"Come I will walk you to the gate. It is getting late," he said, interrupting her thoughts.

"All right. But first let me read the last few lines you wrote."

"At that time, the gods Anu and Enlil, for the enhancement of the well-being of the people, named me by my name: Hammurabi, the pious prince, who venerates the gods, to make justice prevail in the land, to abolish the wicked and the evil, to prevent the strong from oppressing the weak, to rise like the sun-god Šamaš over all humankind, to illuminate the land."

That night Iltani was too wound up to fall asleep. She thought about Marduk-mušallim. She had never known anyone like him before. As a scribe, she occasionally met men here and there, but most of them were family acquaintances. This Marduk-mušallim, he was so different; on the one hand, he radiated confidence, appropriate to his high rank, but there was something else about him, a softness in his demeanor with her. And he was full of joy, boyishly comical, like his bouncing red hair. Iltani fell asleep at last, smiling, dreaming.

Chapter 16

"SO, YOU ARE STILL ALIVE," Awat-Aja said, greeting Iltani. "I thought I might have to start mourning you," she said with a grin. Iltani could see that she was not angry, only teasing.

"You cannot imagine, Awat-Aja. The exhilaration of writing on stone! Marduk-mušallim is unbelievably skillful at it and he is a wonderful teacher. Soon it will be my turn to write on the stele," Iltani said, her eyes wide with elation.

Awat-Aja furrowed her brow. Her eyes narrowed.

"Oh, you worry too much," Iltani said. "It is his ability that I admire him for."

"Are you sure that is all you see in him? I don't want you to get hurt," Awat-Aja said cautiously.

"Yes I am," Iltani said.

"Have you visited your family lately?" Awat-Aja asked, changing the subject.

"No. A visit is long overdue. I have been so busy lately. And what about your brothers? Did you decide to take them to court in the end, or to give your land to someone else?"

"No, that letter we wrote was enough. They are sending me provisions regularly now. We shall see what the future brings, though. Come, the sun is setting, we do not want to be late for Reš-Aja."

All evening while they dined at Reš-Aja's, Iltani's thoughts kept returning to Marduk-mušallim, and she imagined what it would be like to inscribe the great black stele with his eyes on her. It made her shiver. She could hardly eat.

* * *

"I shall have to leave tomorrow. The King sent for me, a matter of some importance," Marduk-mušallim told Iltani at the end of their practice session.

"How long will you stay in Babylon?" Iltani asked.

"Only a few days, I hope. The King knows we are in the middle of our work. I have been keeping him informed."

"Let me know when you return," Iltani said as she left.

"I will. And you should continue to practice."

"I will."

As Iltani walked home, she felt a strange sensation in her stomach. She tried the dismiss it, but without success. Had she missed something? She kept herself occupied, tidying her room and helping Parratum prepare the dinner.

* * *

The next day Iltani chose not to practice, but to devote the day to things she had neglected for some time. She was about to set off on her errands when a messenger arrived to say that *Abu* wished to see her. Iltani had a bad conscience. Several weeks had gone by since her last visit home. She hurried out.

Iltani enjoyed making her way to her childhood home, over the bridges, the sparkling canals, observing all the new houses, the men at work repairing walls, acquaintances passing by. As she approached her street, she noticed the dilapidated state of the houses, including her own. The plaster had peeled off in places and the wooden lintel was rotting. She made a note to speak to Sin-rēmēni about it. Iltani entered the house and found the servant by the stove baking bread. She still expected to see Shima-ahati there, but she was long gone.

"May Šamaš and Aja keep you safe," she said, greeting the new servant and helped herself to a fresh piece of warm bread.

"Iltani, is that you? Come in please," she heard *Abu* call from his library.

She found him sitting with Tabbija's *Abu*, the *asû*-doctor who had treated *Ummu*. *Abu* smiled at her and gestured that she should listen to what the *asû* had to say. Iltani felt awkward, knowing she kept Tabbija's secret from her own father. She avoided looking into his eyes.

"The best thing you can do is to keep her comfortable and give her a potion of thyme soaked in a small amount of beer three times a day. And it would not hurt to make an offering to Gula, goddess of healing, either."

"Thank you. May the gods protect you," *Abu* bid farewell to the *asû* and paid him.

After the *asû* left Iltani hugged *Abu* for a long time.

"Come. Let us go see *Ummu*. She will be so happy to see you," he said.

They went to the big room where *Ummu* lay on a mattress in the dim light of the oil lamps. She looked pale and thin. A thick woolen blanket was tucked around her. Iltani embraced her gently. *Ummu*'s body felt fragile, much thinner then she remembered.

"Iltani, my child, I am so happy to see you," she said feebly.

"How are you, *Ummu*?" Iltani kissed her again.

"Well, I feel weak and cold most of the time and I cannot hold down what I eat. It is this fever that will not go away. But today I have not vomited so far. I will recover. I am not going to my fate just yet. I must help your brother first. Please find him and talk some sense into him."

Iltani searched *Abu*'s face for a clue. He rolled his eyes to signal "later."

"Please call the servant, I must tell her what to prepare for dinner. You will stay with us today, will you not Iltani?" asked *Ummu*.

"Yes, I will," said Iltani. She longed to have a nice long talk with *Abu*, and to see her brother again.

They left *Ummu* to rest and went to *Abu*'s library.

"She does look better today. She will recover," said *Abu* as they entered. "But I thought you should be aware of the situation. Now tell me about yourself; you seem happy. Your work must be keeping you very busy. You have not visited us for such a long time," he added reproachfully.

"I am sorry, but you are right, *Abu*, something truly wondrous has happened to me."

Iltani recounted all that had occurred since King Hammurabi brought the stele into the Šamaš temple. *Abu* listened in amazement. He knew what a talented scribe his daughter was, yet an offer like this was unbelievable.

"And do you know, I met Marduk-mušallim before I entered the *gagû*, here, in this very house, when he came to us with his *Abu* from Babylon. Today he is one of the King's most prominent scribes. He has taught me such a lot. Someday soon, I will show you the part I inscribed."

"Iltani, what an extraordinary thing!" *Abu* said.

"Extraordinarily difficult, too. Look at my poor little finger!" she said, wiggling it.

"By Nabû," *Abu* gently clasped her hand. "How dreadful. Yet you smile?"

"Because I count it a lucky charm. Do not worry on my account, I am no longer in any pain. Now, please *Abu*, tell me, what is this about Sin-rēmēni?" she asked.

"You will have to talk to him yourself. He is usually out for most of the day and *Ummu* disapproves," said *Abu*, still staring in disbelief at Iltani's finger.

"Disapproves of what? Out where?" asked Iltani, hiding her fingers, the source of *Abu*'s concern.

Abu began to pace around.

"Sin-rēmēni, being the youngest, never had many responsibilities at home. And since he lacks patience and discipline, he could not learn the scribal arts. I know, I tried to teach him myself, after he left the É-DUBBA, there was no use. However, he longs to be useful," *Abu* added sadly. "So, you see, as it happened. . ."

"*Abu*, what is it?" Iltani asked impatiently

Abu smiled. "He is an apprentice to a tanner; he skins the sheep and works in leather. He has a natural fitness for this, it seems. The wares he makes are of excellent quality."

"A tanner? How did this come about? Sin-rēmēni, who could not bear to buy fish in the *kārum* because of the smell?" Iltani wrinkled her nose, mimicking her brother. "Why are you smiling, *Abu*?" she asked in confusion.

"Your little brother has fallen in love with the daughter of a tanner," said *Abu* calmly, "and I am glad of it, though *Ummu* disapproves. This girl has wrought a remarkable change in Sin-rēmēni. I have met her and she is good-natured and seems to possess a generous heart. But *Ummu*—she thinks he can do better. She refuses to listen to him and they are hardly speaking these days."

"But how could this girl work such a change in him? I mean, we both know Sin-rēmēni and his delicate nose." Iltani could not understand. Tanners' work occasioned the stench of blood and animal copses in decay.

"I suppose that in giving his heart to her, he chose to become the kind of man she could love and rely on. All this happened at a time when he needed more than anything to prove his worth. The girl's family, the family of Warad-Šamaš, is not so prosperous, although they provide leather to the palace and the temple. Would you be willing to visit Sin-rēmēni there? I know that would make him happy. Go now and come back in time for the evening meal," he suggested, and gave her directions and further information concerning Warad-Šamaš' family. Iltani shuddered at the thought of the tanner's quarter.

"I shall go and meet the lovely ewe who has ensnared Sin-rēmēni, and return in the evening."

* * *

Iltani observed the passersby on her search for Sin-rēmēni. She was not familiar with this quarter of Sippar, located at the far end of the city, near the gate, since the fellmongers and tanners did much of the skinning outside the walls. Their homes were said to reek, yet everyone needed leather, leather for boots and sandals, pouches and belts, shields and harnesses. Most tanners would bring their wares around to the patron's home.

Iltani approached a woman sitting in a courtyard nearby and asked her for directions: "Do you know where the house of Warad-Šamaš is?"

"It is just behind this one," she said, pointing towards a small entrance further down the lane.

Iltani walked in that direction, covering her nose against the smell, which was unbearable. She reached the house and entered the courtyard, where she saw piles of tanned hides, and shoes, sandals and boots of all sizes. In the middle of the courtyard, a stove burning aromatic cypress wood and incense filled the air with fragrance.

Iltani saw the half-naked muscular back of a young man bowed over a piece of leather. An old brown dog lay under a canopy of woven reeds and raised his head and ears slightly at Iltani's approach, then dropped them again. Was that not her brother's dog, Humbaba?

"Excuse me, young sir, is this the house of Warad-Šamaš? I am looking for my brother Sin-rēmēni. I am told he is apprenticing here."

The young man stood up and turned to Iltani. "My sweet sister!"

Iltani was shocked. The last time she had seen her brother, he had been a thin young man, or at least that is how she remembered him. Now he looked much taller and had muscles everywhere.

"Is that really you, Sin-rēmēni?" she asked. "What have you done with my thin little brother?"

"I guess it must be all the hard work and good food," he said, smiling at her. "Come, give me a hug, little sister. You, I see, have shrunk even more."

"Go wash before you come any closer," she cautioned, but lovingly.

"Don't be so sensitive, sister," he said and grinned, while washing his hands and chest with the water from a big basin in the corner and wiping himself dry before throwing on a loose brown tunic.

After a long hug, Sin-rēmēni invited her into the house. The room was spread with softest leather and woolen rugs. He served her beer and apples. Humbaba followed them in, sniffed at Iltani, rubbed against her and then lay down, breathing heavily.

"He can hardly see or smell anymore, poor old Humbaba. I am afraid he will soon go to his fate. So what are you doing here, did *Ummu* send you?"

Iltani did not respond, but merely asked where everyone of this household was.

"Warad-Šamaš, my master, is felling hides outside the walls where there is a big storage house for tanners. What you smell around here is nothing compared to the stench out there."

Iltani did not dare to imagine that.

"And Warad-Šamaš's wife and daughter are down by the river washing clothes," he said.

"Would you please explain what you are doing here?" Iltani finally asked. "Why would the son of a scribe want to become a tanner? I promise not to judge you, but I need to understand. You know that I am not like *Ummu*," she said, observing him tenderly. With Sin-rēmēni she need never beat around the bush, she knew. She could always say what was on her mind.

"I had to find my own path in life. I lack the persistence to become a scribe, as everyone knows, so I tried working here and there, hoping to achieve something. *Ummu* does not know it, but *Abu* helped me out many times. Then Warad-Šamaš hired me for a day's work at the tannery outside of the city. That is how I met his daughter Sabitum. She came to help her father load the hides on the wagon. Before long, all I cared about was being with Sabitum. At the beginning, I kept it a secret from everyone in the family. Later, I thought that she would be welcomed at our house, but *Ummu* would not hear of it. So I asked Warad-Šamaš to take me in as an apprentice, just so I could be close to Sabitum. He said he could not afford to pay a full apprentice, but I convinced him anyhow, and promised to work for free at first. That was almost five months ago. As you see, I have learned the trade. You may find it hard to believe, but I actually enjoy the hard work. At last, I have a skill. I want to show you some of my wares here: boots and sandals and delicate slippers. I will make a pair especially for you. Warad-Šamaš is better off since I started working for him. He has no sons, so I am like a son to him. He knows of my wish to. . ." Sin-rēmēni stopped and looked at Iltani who listening closely, "marry his daughter."

Iltani could not help but see that her brother was radiantly happy as part of the tanner's family.

"Sin-rēmēni? Are you there?" They heard a voice call and a young woman entered the courtyard, delicate, almost fragile looking, with luminous eyes and long brown hair. Her full smiling lips spread a feeling of happiness.

"Come, I will introduce you," said Sin-rēmēni, and introduced her to Sabitum. Iltani saw the way he gazed at her, almost worshipfully. His eye glowed and Sabitum's eyes reflected the glow.

"It is getting late," said Iltani after they had spoken for a while. "I must return to *Abu* and *Ummu*'s house for the evening meal."

"Here, I want you to try these on." Sin-rēmēni gave Iltani a pair of sandals.

"If you like them perhaps some of the other *nadītu* will want to buy some too. We would deliver them to the *gagû* gate, free of charge." He shamelessly promoted his wares.

Sin-rēmēni accompanied her part of the way home.

"Thank you, my brother. May Šamaš and Aja keep you both healthy," she said, blessing him and Sabitum as she left. "I am very happy for you my little brother."

"Thank you, beloved sister, this means very much to me."

They parted and Iltani went back to her parent's house. She was thankful to see *Ummu* looking much stronger. Iltani and *Abu* spoke mainly about scribal matters over the meal. Then *Abu* escorted her back to the *gagû*.

"So what do you think about your brother?" *Abu* asked.

"I think he has done very well for himself. He is happy. And Sabitum is lovely as can be."

"I agree. *Ummu* will come around. She will be glad to see Sin-rēmēni happy."

"As far as I can see, his future family will prosper thanks to him. Trust Sin-rēmēni," said Iltani with a hug in parting from *Abu* at the gate.

Back in her room, she thought about Sin-rēmēni, that he was willing to give up the comforts of a wealthy home and work hard just to be close to the girl he loved. Was she like that, too, in her quest to become a scribe many years ago? Was it the same kind of feeling?

* * *

The next morning Iltani took a pouch of barley to the Šamaš temple. The new sandals were smooth and comfortable, stronger than her old pair, with a thicker sole and straps that held her feet more snugly. She thought about Sin-rēmēni, about how unfathomable life can be. He, the son of a scribe, had never considered becoming a tanner and making sandals, yet the gods had somehow directed him to that path where he found success. "Just as I was meant to become a scribe," she thought.

She also kept thinking about the black stone. She imagined the first time she would place the chisel on the stone and swing the hammer lightly, engraving into the black diorite. The image thrilled her. She thought about Marduk-mušallim; she missed his company.

A few days later, a messenger came by to say that Marduk-mušallim expected Iltani to join him the following morning. Iltani was elated. She could hardly wait to see him again.

Next morning, as she dressed herself, Iltani felt the strange fluttering in her stomach. She was so agitated; Parratum asked if anything was wrong. On her way from the *gagû* to the Šamaš-temple, she imagined seeing Marduk-mušallim's face again, the moment of their reunion. Why was she so nervous? And what was wrong with her stomach?

When she arrived at the High Priest's court, she saw him right away, and her breath came fast. He was reading the script on the stone. She tried to calm herself: "May Šamaš and Aja keep you in good health," she greeted him from afar. He turned around and beamed at her. "It is good to see you, Iltani." She almost sighed with relief. "I hope you have been practicing," he said. "Tomorrow you begin."

Chapter 17

"I SENT EVERYONE ELSE AWAY," said Marduk-mušallim. There was tension in his voice.

"Thank you," Iltani said. "But do not fear. A girl can be as good a scribe as any man, remember?" she said in a tone of self-mockery to steady herself. She took a deep breath and concentrated on the tools in her hands, their angle and position. No room for error.

As she tapped the chisel with the hammer a charge went through her body like a burst of fire. She continued to inscribe, oblivious to her surroundings. It was she, Iltani, and King Hammurabi's stele.

Marduk-mušallim watched like a proud father. She was the very best scribe he had ever seen.

Iltani work quietly, stopping only for an occasional sip of water.

In silent amazement Marduk-mušallim watched her hands, her elegance of movement. "You are even better than I expected," he said at the day's end.

Iltani was thoroughly exhausted after these hours of physical and mental effort. Her head felt light, but she was happy with her achievement.

"Thank you for allowing me this opportunity, Marduk-mušallim. I am deeply grateful to you. Becoming a scribe has not been without difficulties, but today is the greatest reward of all."

"This day is one of the happiest in my life too," Marduk-mušallim said, looking directly into Iltani's eyes. The sun began to set, but neither of them moved. They sat together drinking beer, and gazing at the shining black stone.

* * *

Within a few weeks, Iltani had finished carving her section of the stone. Nevertheless, she continued to come to the inner court almost every day. She felt so happy in Marduk-mušallim's company, watching the progress on the inscription and discussing various things with him. She enjoyed watching him, his movements, his back, his hands, and most of all his bouncing, burning red curls.

By Elul the work was complete. The King arrived for the official unveiling of the stele. Iltani was there too, watching from the side. Marduk-mušallim had wanted to introduce her to the King and his son, Prince Samsu-iluna, but Iltani had declined. She wanted to stay in the background.

"I must see you tomorrow morning, before I leave for Babylon," Marduk-mušallim told her at the end of the ceremony. "Can you meet me in the High Priest's court? I will be packing."

"Yes, I can. I will come," Iltani said, as she wondered what this was about.

On her way home that night, Iltani was overcome with a kind of sadness. She had spent so much time with him, more than she had with anyone before. She painfully understood: she would miss him, her friend, Marduk-mušallim, not just their work together.

* * *

"I bought you a gift while I was in Babylon," Marduk-mušallim said, handing her a soft bundle. "Here, this is for you, the present is inside."

Iltani sat down, untied the knotted string and removed the cloth.

"By Šamaš and Aja!" she exclaimed. "This is too much." Inside was a magnificent necklace of gold and large lapis lazuli beads on a fine piece of soft cotton weave with purple stripes.

"Let me put it on you," Marduk-mušallim said, helping her up. He stood behind her, gently moving her hair aside to clasp the necklace.

"Marduk-mušallim, this necklace is beautiful and so is the cloth. But why are you giving me all this? You have paid me well for my work," she said, as she faced him.

Marduk-mušallim looked into Iltani's eyes. He was hesitant, searching for the right words.

"What is it?" Iltani asked.

"Iltani, I want you to leave the *gagû* and become my wife," he said, trembling. "I love you more than I have ever loved anyone. I have wanted you for a long time now. You are my, challenger." He stopped, searching her eyes for the answer he hoped for.

Iltani could not speak.

"I know I am asking something forbidden. You are a *nadītu* of Šamaš, but I am the King's scribe, I will find a way to free you."

Iltani was confused. "I do not need to be freed, I am no captive."

"Do you not want to go with me to Babylon and be my wife? We belong together, that is what the gods have ordained, that is what I know in my heart, and you, Iltani, do you not know it too?" Marduk-mušallim pleaded with his eyes.

Iltani began to understand, all that time, working at his side, watching him move, the pleasure of being with him, was that love?

"But *Abu* always told me that my path in life was to become a scribe and a *nadītu* of Šamaš, that is what I always wanted, nothing else. That is my destiny, that is what the gods have ordained for me. I enjoy your company and you are a great scribe and teacher, Marduk-mušallim, but I am content with my life as it is."

"I am more than a scribe, I am a man, and although you are a *nadītu*, you are still a woman. People change. Desires change. Do you feel no desire to be with me, to see me and hold me?" Marduk-mušallim asked despairingly.

Iltani hesitated. She had never thought seriously about the love of a man. She loved her family, but this was something else—the excitement she felt when she saw him, the fluttering in her stomach. Was that enough to make her leave the life she knew? She tried to answer as truthfully as she could.

"It is a joy to work with you, Marduk-mušallim. You have taught me so much, you are close to my heart, you are my friend and I know I will miss you. But I cannot leave the *gagû*, the only place where I can live the life of a scribe, not a woman with a husband and children and a household to run."

"Iltani," Marduk-mušallim's voice was filled with pain now. "I would never ask you to give up being a scribe; there is no reason for that. No law prohibits a married woman from working as a scribe. You, we would find a way for you to continue teaching and scribing. Iltani," he took her hands and held them gently, "I have known the pain of losing someone I cared for, and there is no greater pain. I believe that you have feelings of love for me, I can feel it. Please, please, come with me, tie your life with mine. I need you. We will be happy. I will provide for you, I will always love you and keep you safe, as safe as you are in the *gagû*."

"I do care for you, I care for you greatly, Marduk-mušallim. But I cannot leave. My life is here," Iltani said sorrowfully.

Marduk-mušallim stood quietly, his smile gone, his eyes despondent.

"Thank you for these beautiful gifts. I must leave now. I will miss you. You have been my greatest teacher. May Šamaš and Aja keep you safe forever."

Iltani drew closer and hugged him. She felt his strength, his arms embracing her, not letting her go. It was the first time she had ever been so close to a man outside her family. His hands made her body burn. She had to go. She pulled away and left him standing there. She did not look back, but she could feel his eyes on her, watching as she walked away.

* * *

"What is it, Iltani?" Awat-Aja asked. "You look dreadful."

Iltani rose from her cushion and walked over to the reed-hamper. She took out the cloth and necklace and displayed it to Awat-Aja.

"He gave me these, and then he asked me to leave the *gagû* and become his wife." Iltani spoke as in a trance.

"What?" her friend let out a cry. "What did you answer?" she asked with trepidation.

"I said no."

Both *nadītu* were silent for a while.

"Do you wish to talk about it?" Awat-Aja broke the silence.

"No. What is there to say? This is where I belong. I am the best female scribe in the *gagû*. That is my life," Iltani answered.

Awat-Aja wanted to asked Iltani what she really felt, but she held her tongue.

"You tried to warn me once. I had no idea he felt like this, poor Marduk-mušallim," Iltani said, gazing at the air.

"I am sorry for your friend's pain," Awat-Aja said, more concerned about the pain Iltani would soon be feeling. Marduk-mušallim clearly loved Iltani, and Iltani, she sensed, loved him in return, without realizing it.

* * *

After the evening meal, Iltani lay awake on her mattress. She had made the right decision, she was certain of it. True, she liked Marduk-mušallim very much, but that

172

was no reason to leave the *gagû*, and the life she had built for herself, the position of respect she had earned as a fine scribe and teacher. How could she give it up to be a wife? Here in the *gagû* she was her own mistress.

"But why then, why is this so hard for me and so confusing?" she pondered out loud.

She slept restlessly and was awakened before dawn by Parratum.

"I am sorry to wake you, Mistress Iltani, but the gatekeeper is here. He says there is someone with an urgent message for you."

Iltani dressed herself and washed her face. It was still dark outside, and the gatekeeper stood outside holding a candle.

"The King's scribe awaits you at the gate. He said it was urgent."

"Tell him I will come, thank you," Iltani dismissed the gatekeeper. It must be Marduk-mušallim, she thought.

She walked to the gate, shivering with apprehension. The sun was rising slowly. Had she made the wrong decision? Would she miss him more then she could bear? As she walked through the gate, under the gatekeeper's gaze, she saw Marduk-mušallim holding the reins of his horse. She walked towards him. His smile was sad. He looked tired.

"I am on my way back to Babylon. I needed to see you one more time before I leave. Please Iltani, be my wife. Change your mind, and together we will remove away all obstacles. I promise you a good life, a life of love."

Iltani could hardly breathe. She felt more for him than she was willing to admit.

"I am sorry, Marduk-mušallim. I am sorry but my life is here, and it is complete. I will miss you, I know, but I cannot leave. It would be wrong to change my destiny."

Iltani felt tears streaming down as she uttered the words. She turned away and ran back to the *gagû*.

Marduk-mušallim watched her disappear within the walls; he mounted his horse and rode away.

* * *

The wedding took place a few weeks after Marduk-mušallim's departure. Iltani joined her own family and the family of the bride. *Abu* looked happy, in contrast to *Ummu*, who seemed dissatisfied. Iltani guessed she had not reconciled with Sin-rēmēni, but Sin-rēmēni was radiant. He could not stop looking at Sabitum, his bride.

Food and beer were served, with bread and sesame oil, dried fruit and roasted fish. Three lyre players and a drummer played wedding songs. The bride's dowry was small: leatherwear, two wooden chairs, several lengths of cloth and five small jars of scented oil. The groom's family received four pairs of sandals, a jug of oil and several storage jars.

Iltani caught Sin-rēmēni and pulled him aside.

"I want to ask you something, little brother. I see how happy you are. How did you know that Sabitum was the right girl for you? Did it not matter to you that her family is poor? Or that you would have to change your way of life?"

"My dear sister. I knew the moment I saw her, but even so, working with her family and getting to know her better made me see that this is what my life should be. You always knew you wanted to become a scribe. Only when I met Sabitum did I realize that what is most important to me is being with someone I love. That is what makes me complete. I could not rest until I made certain that I would see her every day. I do not care that I am not a scribe. I actually like being a tanner. I am pleased, just as I am."

"I wish you luck, my dear brother. I cannot wait to visit you both."

"We are truly blessed by the gods, all of us. You are fulfilling your dreams and I have found mine. *Ummu* will come around. *Abu* thinks so too. She is afraid of poverty because she grew up poor. I will not be poor. I am good at my trade and I am building up Warad-Šamaš's business. But all that is insignificant. What matters is that I found Sabitum and I am profoundly happy."

Iltani hugged him and Sabitum and the other members of her family. She was ready to leave. A servant escorted her home. She thought about Marduk-mušallim. Surely, had she not been a *nadītu*, she would have accepted his offer of marriage. But she was happy in her life, why change it? She had been right to refuse him. She belonged in the *gagû*.

The next morning, after bringing her offering to the gods, she made arrangements to see her pupils again. It was time to return to her former life, to fill it with work.

Chapter 18

IT WAS KISLÎMU, ALMOST THREE MONTHS since Marduk-mušallim returned to Babylon. The days were shorter and darker and at night there was a chill in the air.

Reluctantly, Iltani admitted to herself that something, or rather, someone was missing. She used to be happy, content with the routine of scribing, teaching and praying. Now, every morning was gloomier than the morning before and every evening was emptier. She had lost all interest in her work. Her usually friendly disposition turned sour and impatient, even hostile sometimes.

She longed for the excitement she had felt with Marduk-mušallim.

The walls of the *gagû*, which had once betokened pride, security, rank, and privilege, seemed to be closing in on her, isolating her from another life, a life with Marduk-mušallim. She was suffering, just as Marduk-mušallim had predicted.

* * *

"Did you practice at all? This is not worth the clay it is written on," Iltani said, raising her voice at her pupil and threw the tablet into a water basin. "You will start from the beginning again. Go, go home. That is all for today."

What did those girls think? That they could achieve something without practice? So she gave them a lot of home practice. She had worked so hard at their age her fingers were always full of cuts; those girls were petulant children, spoiled rotten. But were they really? As if two people in her head were locked in a dispute about whether

176

the girls were really spoiled or whether she perhaps had lost her patience.

* * *

"I cannot talk about it, Awat-Aja, please," Iltani said over the evening meal with her friend. "There is nothing you can say or do. You warned me and now I must suffer the consequence. It will pass. I will become myself again and forget about him."

Awat-Aja was not convinced. She knew Iltani well enough to have seen the change in her friend while she worked with Marduk-mušallim, and the difference after he left. Iltani had never looked so miserable. Nothing brought her joy anymore. What if she stayed like that forever? Awat-Aja worried.

"Could you teach me something new, or could we read together?" she asked. Teaching and reading had always brightened Iltani's mood in the past.

"No. I am tired. You can read by yourself. I want to go home. Thank you for the meal," Iltani said brusquely.

"Iltani, it will pass. You will be your old self again. I understand your pain," Awat-Aja made a last attempt to comfort her friend.

"I know you mean well. Good night," Iltani answered. She felt it would never pass. The pain was too strong. Living apart from him; knowing she had made the wrong choice. Nothing her friend said helped in the least.

* * *

"Mistress Iltani. I am going to buy fish for tonight's meal, is there anything else you want?" Parratum called from the courtyard.

"Wait for me. I will come with you," she said. The weather was mild for this time of year. She thought it might be pleasant to walk and think of other things.

"I want to walk down to the river. I will meet you back home," Iltani said as they reached the lane of the fishmongers.

The water glimmered grey-blue. Iltani stood at the quay. Two caracoles, tied to a pole, were rocking to the rhythm of the waves. A little further down, she saw two young women washing clothes. Her gaze wandered aimlessly over the bank, and suddenly stopped; she panicked at what she saw. It was him, she recognized him from afar, Marduk-mušallim, standing on the riverbank. It cannot be, she thought. She battled the impulse to run away, but though she tried to, her body froze like a statue. Her heart raced. His wild red curls consumed her like flames.

And then she saw Marduk-mušallim pick up the young child who emerged from the cold water. The woman standing next to them laughed and threw a cloth over the child to dry him off. They were a family, his family. Iltani did not understand it.

She heard a loud cry, the cry of a wounded animal, and looked around for the source of the sound; she noticed everyone was staring at her. She was the one who was screaming. When she looked again in Marduk-mušallim's direction, their eyes met. He stared fixedly at her with his beautiful eyes, neither moving nor paying attention to the little boy who was tugging at his arm. In that brief moment when they were locked in each other's gaze, the world around them ceased to exist. But the boy kept pulling Marduk-mušallim's arm firmly until he looked at him and broke the connection with Iltani.

There he was with his wife and son. He had misled her. All she had felt these last few months was a sham. She regained control of her limbs and started to walk, and then run, away from the unbearable source of her agony. She did not hear a voice calling her name, or see Marduk-mušallim hug the child, say a few words to the woman and run after her.

Iltani ran with no sense of direction. How could she have been so wrong, so deceived? She stopped running and wondered where to go. To see her brother Sin-rēmēni and his new wife, she decided.

Exhausted, she arrived at his courtyard. Sin-rēmēni saw her and ran to catch her just as she collapsed. She did not answer his questions, but only assured him no one had caused her physical harm. She lay on a mattress inside and cried until she fell asleep.

When Iltani woke up it was almost dark. The smell of cooking filled the air. She stood up and found Sin-rēmēni and Sabitum snuggled together by the fire.

"Thank you both for your hospitality. May Šamaš and Aja repay you. Could you please escort me home?"

"Do you not wish to stay with us till morning? You can sleep here, my sister," Sin-rēmēni said, taking her hand.

"My servant will worry about me; no one knows I am here," Iltani said.

"I will run and tell the gatekeeper to inform your servant. Sabitum will give you whatever you need for the night." And he ran off, before Iltani could protest.

After the evening meal, the young couple made sure Iltani was comfortable on one of the mattresses and left her to herself, dividing the room with a long curtain.

Iltani lay awake going over and over what she had seen. Could it be? Only a few months ago, he had asked her to marry him and be his wife. Did he want a second wife? That was unusual, especially when there was already a child. Iltani felt hurt, confused, and angry. She tossed and turned for a long time before she fell sleep.

* * *

"I love you, I want you to go to Babylon with me and leave the *gagû*. Be my wife, have my children, Iltani." And he kissed her very gently, taking her hands, placing them on his heart. Iltani, apprehensive by this intimacy, wanted to step back, but instead she felt her body move closer and closer, his arms clasping her tightly, his lips passionately kissing hers. Her mind was confused, but it was ecstasy. She drew closer and closer, she was burning . . . and then she let go of all reserve and her mind obeyed her body; she grasped his curls and pulled him to her, responding passionately to his kisses, moaning with desire. . .

* * *

"Iltani, Iltani, are you all right? You were moving and moaning in your sleep." Sabitum touched her lightly on the shoulder.

Iltani looked at her, realizing it was just a dream. A wonderful, hopeless dream. She gasped for breath and Sabitum called Sin-rēmēni for help.

"Should I fetch the *asû*?" he asked.

"No, no *asû*," Iltani whispered, trying to control her breathing. "I will tell you everything." She asked for something warm to drink, and then they all sat down and listened. Iltani told them how she and Marduk-mušallim had met, and about the marriage proposal she had declined. Only after he left, she realized how much she loved him. She wished she had accepted. She was even willing to give up being a *nadītu*.

"And then I saw him by the river yesterday, with a child and a woman," she said with grief.

Sin-rēmēni and Sabitum were speechless. They had not expected such a story.

"Can I help in some way?" Sin-rēmēni asked quietly.

"No. There is nothing you can do. Only, please do not talk about this to anyone. I have to get to the *gagû*. It is morning. Do not worry about me." Sin-rēmēni looked at Sabitum and she nodded.

"I will escort you back."

They walked in silence. Iltani was lost in thought.

"Please Sin-rēmēni, we are almost at the gate, let me walk alone from here."

Sin-rēmēni hugged her. "I will send a messenger to ask about your health. I am your brother and I love you very much. Please let me know what you need and I will do whatever I can. You are always welcome in our house, no matter what hour of the day or night." He looked at her and smiled: "If you like, I will find your Marduk-mušallim and give him a sound thrashing. I am very strong you know," he said half seriously.

"No, please do not. Thank you my dear brother. Go to your kind and lovely wife, cherish every moment with her," Iltani said mournfully.

* * *

As Iltani approached the *gagû*, the gatekeeper ran toward her. "Iltani, I have a very important message for you. Yesterday one of the King's scribes was here, Marduk-mušallim. He waited for you almost the whole day. He said he needed to talk to you on a matter of great urgency but he was gone by the time your brother reported your whereabouts."

Iltani heard the guard's words, but she was too bewildered to respond. She went home, washed, and changed her clothes, intending to walk to the temple and pray, but just as she finished her morning meal, a messenger ran into the courtyard.

"The chief scribe needs to see you immediately and I am to bring you to him."

"What is this about?" Iltani asked warily.

"He did not say. Please come. It is imperative." Iltani considered taking her reed stylus with her. She could hardly think. What did the chief scribe need her for so early in the morning?

"I do not feel very well. Could you send my apologies to the scribe?" she asked the messenger.

"He said that you must come without delay," he said sternly.

"All right," Iltani said reluctantly.

* * *

As they approached the gate to the Šamaš–temple and climbed the stairs, she had a sinking feeling. Had this anything to do with Marduk-mušallim? She entered the chief scribe's chambers and saw him standing in the courtyard. Memories of Marduk-mušallim surfaced painfully.

"Ah, Iltani. An urgent matter has come up. I need the best female scribe."

Iltani sighed with relief. So, he needed her services, that was all. No secrets would be revealed.

"A most noble lady visiting from Larsa needs a letter and she sent a messenger this morning requesting the best female scribe to be brought to her. She is the wife of an important official in King Hammurabi's court. You must go directly there. Take some clay from my hamper and a stylus if you need one. Here," he handed her a small basket, "take this."

* * *

Iltani was hardly able to concentrate in her present state. Her mind was in turmoil. She would try to do her best. The messenger led her to the noble lady's residence and left her there. Iltani walked through the courtyard, ready to greet the lady with the blessing of Šamaš and Aja, when suddenly she saw Marduk-mušallim and the child. He was showing him a tablet.

"Iltani," he said, jumping up, his red curls flying in all directions. Before she could run away again, he grabbed the boy's hand and approached Iltani.

"Iltani, I want you to meet my son Šamaš-bani," he said, smiling fearfully.

Iltani was speechless. So looked at his weary face, at the black circles under his eyes. She heard the words he spoke, but what did they mean? Why had he brought her here under false pretenses? What did he want from her?

Iltani heard a woman's voice. "Marduk-mušallim, Šamaš-bani would like to go for a walk, may I take him?" said the woman she had seen yesterday by the river.

"Yes, please *Abu!*" the boy pleaded.

"Yes. Enjoy yourselves. Take your time."

Iltani watched them walk away. Only she and Marduk-mušallim were left in the courtyard.

"Please, Iltani, do not run away again until you hear all I have to tell you," he said softly. "Come, let us talk inside," he said, pointing to the entrance of a room.

Iltani followed him, afraid of being misled again. Afraid of what was about to come.

Inside the room, Marduk-mušallim motioned for her to sit down on a cushion, but Iltani declined.

"I will stand," were the first words she was able to utter.

Marduk-mušallim nodded tensely and stood facing her on the other side of the room.

"Forgive me for luring you here under false pretenses, but this is the only time I have ever lied to you. Please, hear me out before you judge me. Do not vanish again." He waited for a response, but Iltani merely looked at him. He continued: "I can only imagine what you thought when you saw us by the river yesterday, a man, a woman, and a young child. The boy is my son, it is true, but the woman is neither my wife nor the mother of my child. My wife died in childbirth. The woman is my son's caretaker. I never told you about him, because. . ." he seemed to search for the right answer, "I was afraid that a child would deter you. But you refused me even before I had a chance to tell you about my son."

Iltani's head was spinning. Could she trust her own judgment?

"Why did you come to Sippar?" she asked diffidently.

"I. . ." Marduk-mušallim weighed his words. "I. . ." And without a warning he approached Iltani and took her hands. "I have come for you. Only for you. I had to know whether you changed your mind. I cannot stop thinking of you. I have been alone since my wife died. I had many offers of marriage, but avoided them, each time with a different pretext. And then I met you, my beautiful scribe. I fell in love with you." His beseeching eyes rested on Iltani's face. "And I know you love me too. If not, would you have run away yesterday? Please, Iltani, change your mind, come with me, be my wife."

Iltani, overwhelmed by her feelings, a mixture of fear, and doubt, concealed her face with her hands.

She trembled as he held her to his heart. Were the gods giving her a second chance? Perhaps she had declined the first time in order to feel her loneliness without him, to find out how much she loved and yearned for him. But could she live with the consequences of her choice now?

"What about the loss of the home I have known for the last nine years? The loss of my status as a *nadītu*?" She uttered one question after the other, mostly to herself.

Marduk-mušallim held Iltani close and stroked her hair. Slowly he leaned over and whispered to her, "You must be scared, afraid of this leap into the unknown. I promise I will love and protect you. Have courage. I cannot bear to lose you again."

He kissed her ear softly and then her cheek. She felt his kisses as through a fog. Slowly his lips sought hers and he kissed her tenderly, then pulled away just enough to look into her eyes.

He held her head between his hands, his eyes pleading: "Be my wife, Iltani. Join your destiny with mine."

At that moment Iltani knew. There was nothing in the world more powerful than her love for this man. Her destiny she was groomed for must have changed. The gods must approve. She looked into his eyes, anxiously awaiting her answer and yet luminous and gentle.

"I will take you as my husband," she said. She was floating.

Marduk-mušallim, now ecstatic, kissed Iltani first moderately, but his desire and yearning for Iltani erupted and his kisses became more passionate, pressing.

When Iltani pulled away to gasp for air, they both began to laugh and the tension eased.

"I promise I will make you the happiest wife in Babylon," Marduk-mušallim whispered, caressing her face, his face nestling in the crook of her neck.

"But what about your son? What if he does not like me?" Iltani asked.

Marduk-mušallim raised his head and looked at Iltani. He held her hands. She leaned against the wall as he embraced her again. She was his willing captive now.

"You will be a wife, my wife. That comes with new challenges, learning to be a mother. But could that be harder than learning to be a scribe? Or to master the challenge of inscribing on the stele of the King. . . ?" He winked at her. He had to stop talking because Iltani freed herself from his grip and covered his mouth with her hand.

She remembered her delirious reverie the night before; she wanted a peek at her new life. "I have no doubt that you will teach me to be a wife as well as you taught me to write on stone," she said, kissing him with the ecstasy she remembered from the dream.

A bit later Iltani took his hand and said firmly, "Now we must go and speak to *Abu*."

* * *

"What do you mean? Oh *Abu*, how can you deny me?" Iltani asked.

"A *nadītu* cannot leave the *gagû*, it is the law," *Abu* said angrily. "I raised you to be a *nadītu* and a scribe, and that is what you always wanted to be for as long as I can remember. That has always been your destiny. And who are you?" he turned to Marduk-mušallim," to think you can change the laws? You should have left without a backward glance. I will never agree to this. My daughter is a *nadītu* and will remain so for the rest of her life."

* * *

185

Iltani had never heard *Abu* speak like this before, so angry and unshakable. She was stunned and wounded by his reaction.

"But *Abu*, do you not want me to be happy?"

"You are happy in the *gagû*, and you always have been. That is where you belong."

"If it is a question of the bridal gift and dowry, I will comply with your wishes, happily," Marduk-mušallim said in a confidential tone, alluding to a sensitive subject. "I have an honorable position in the King's court and I am handsomely paid in land and property. I will settle the account with the *gagû*, if they require compensation."

"Even if the priests agree, and I am not sure they will, do you know what people will say about me, about my family? This is an outrage. My neighbor whose daughter ran away from the *gagû* with a servant is a laughingstock. And what about my daughter's career as a scribe? She has worked too hard to achieve her status to give it up now and become a mother to your child," *Abu* fumed.

"Your daughter is the most gifted scribe I have ever known. She will be my wife, but she will never stop being a scribe, I will make sure of that," Marduk-mušallim said firmly.

"*Abu*," Iltani said in pain. "Ever since I was a little girl you have told me that it is my destiny to be a scribe and a *nadītu*. I was young; I believed every word you said. I have never sought the love of a man or marriage, but I found it. I am not a child. I have been my own mistress for a long time and the destiny you elected for me has changed. The gods changed it. I will marry Marduk-mušallim—it is their will, as well as mine."

"Well I see you have made up your minds." *Abu* stood up. "There is nothing more to say now, I must go," he said, leaving everyone in a state of uncertainty.

* * *

Marduk-mušallim walked with Iltani to the *gagû* gate, keeping a distance for the sake of propriety, only lightly brushing her hand from time to time.

"Do you want to change your mind? Your *Abu* will raise difficulties for us and it will not go smoothly," Marduk-mušallim asked, his voice anxious.

"I did not expect him to object so strongly, or to object at all, in fact. I thought he wanted for me to be happy, but I see now that it was more than that. He wanted the honor I could bring to the family, that was at the top of the list, and my happiness came second. Now I am a full grown woman and I understand that being just a scribe is not enough anymore. I will be your wife."

"Then tomorrow I will speak to the High Priest and we shall see what needs to be done," he said, looking into her eyes. "Whatever lies ahead, we will work it through together. I promise you. Good night. Until tomorrow," he said, waving an imperceptible kiss as she entered the *gagû* and walked straight to Awat-Aja's house.

* * *

Awat-Aja was astonished to hear the news.

"Will the *gagû* let you go, just like that?"

"Probably not. I may have to ask the Princess for help."

"Should I talk to Reš-Aja?" Awat-Aja offered.

"No. Let us wait and we see what happens tomorrow. He is the King's scribe, after all. And there is one more thing. I want to give you my tablets so you can carry on teaching my pupils, especially Lamassani," Iltani said.

"You instructed me how to read and write, but I am no teacher," her friend protested.

"This Lamassani is having a difficult time. She reminds me a little of you when you first arrived. You would be helping a sister *nadītu*. And you could also teach the girls the art of dressing well," Iltani teased her friend. "You do remember how much studying together helped us both."

187

"All right. But you will have to pay me in letters and write to me at least once a month. I will miss you very much," Awat-Aja said, deeply saddened.

"I will miss you too, my sister. I am frightened of the unknown, of feeling helpless again."

"Do not forget that you will have a husband."

"Yes I know, but I am not sure, what that will be like?"

"You will just have to learn as you go along."

* * *

"Wake up, Mistress." Parratum jolted Iltani out of a dream. "The King's scribe awaits you at the gate. The gatekeeper was just here."

Iltani sat up. "Is it morning already?"

"Almost."

"Thank you, Parratum," Iltani said. "I will get dressed."

What was so urgent? Something must have happened, Iltani thought as she hurried to the gate.

Marduk-mušallim was waiting for her there, reins in hand. Behind him stood the King's horsemen and a company of soldiers.

"Iltani." Marduk-mušallim approached and lowered his voice, almost to a whisper. "Etel-pī-Maruduk, the commander of the troops in Sippar, received this letter late last night." He handed her a small clay tablet to read.

"To Etel-pī-Maruduk say, thus says Sumsu-iluna. My father, the King is ill and I have seated myself on the dynastic throne in order to provide justice throughout the land. As soon as you read my letter, you and the elders of the province under your administration are to come at once to Babylon!"

"What does this mean?" Iltani asked.

"We are betrothed and we shall be married. But we will have to wait," Marduk-mušallim said seriously. "I will write to you. I am truly sorry I have to leave now. I love you," he said, and before Iltani could protest, he kissed her passionately, and pressed her to his heart.

"I will come for you as soon as I can. Wait for my letter."

* * *

Iltani watched bewilderedly as the cavalry disappeared, heading south for Babylon.

Epilogue

"To Iltani say, thus (says) Marduk-mušallim. May Šamaš, Marduk and Nabu keep you safe. The land of the black-headed has a new King, Sumsu-iluna. I am close to him, as you know, a friend. He grieves for his father. His advisers warn of a rebel camp, insurgents conquered by his father, King Hammurabi. For now, the land is safe. I have permission to leave within a week. We must hurry.

"Has your *Abu* changed his mind? I will bring gold and gifts for your family and the *gagû*. I have a letter for the Princess from Sumsu-iluna; she is the new King's aunt now, after all. I am certain she can help us. I need you here with me, in Babylon, Iltani. Please do not change your mind. I miss you very much. May the gods keep you safe."

* * *

Iltani held the tablet to her heart. Then she read it over and over. Had *Abu* changed his mind? No. He would not hear of the marriage and threatened to cut her off from her inheritance. But it mattered very little. She had made the right decision this time. She loved Marduk-mušallim and he loved her. But will that be enough? Her strong feeling for him? Will the *gagû* consent to letting her go? Will the Princess really have the power to help?

Iltani stood there with no answers. She raised her head to the sky, looking at the top of the Ziggurat, and prayed.

Author's note

In the beginning of the nineteenth century, adventurers and intellectuals from the West were fascinated with the hidden treasures and secrets of the Orient. In Mesopotamia- the land between the Euphrates and the Tigris (Iraq of today), the great ruins of the Ziggurat alluded to the story of the tower of Babel in the Bible and set their imagination on fire. Their quest for learning about those ancient countries and languages brought about the findings of ancient cities and the deciphering of the long dead cuneiform script. Today hundreds of thousands of those ancient artifacts from Mesopotamia are safely kept in museums around the world, for the general population to see and the scholars to study.

In general it may be worth noting that while *She Wrote on Clay* is, of course, fictional, I based as many parts as possible on archeological findings, especially written documents, and historical facts. The following texts and artifacts have been a great inspiration for me while writing the story.

The Hammurabi code

The beautiful black diorite stone was inscribed during the reign of King Hammurabi between ca.1792 to 1750 BCE. In the twelfth century BCE, it was taken as booty by the Elamite king Shutruk-Nahhunte to the ancient city of Susa (Persian), where it was found in an archeological excavation in 1901 CE and brought to the Louvre. Many scholars believe that it was originally erected in the city of Sippar.

The stone was inscribed with ca. 282 "law provisions" which are framed by a prologue and epilogue. Whether the inscribed were verdicts or laws, is still debated by the scholars, as well as its use in the day to day legal procedures.

The Hammurabi code was not the only "law code" inscribed in the history of the Ancient Near East, but it is the most famous one, even during its own time. Many fractional copies of the Hammurabi code were found, and it was learned in scribal schools even long after Hammurabi and his dynasty was gone. Since it was found, it has yielded many scholarly studies and was translated into many languages e.g. English, German, French and Hebrew.

For further reading and Bibliography see:
http://en.wikipedia.org/wiki/Code_of_Hammurabi

The *nadītu* and the *gagû*

An abundant number of texts shed light on the economic activities of the *nadītu* women in Sippar and in other cities, supplemented by letters with further information about their family relations, especially with their brothers.

Scholars are not in agreement as to why in the Old Babylonian period the *gagû* became a larger institution than the years before. Some scholars assume that it was an economic development. Since more people had started to own private land and property, it was one way to preserve the family's capital. If the daughter got married, some of the family's property may have been given to the daughter's new family, while if she became a *nadītu*, the property mostly stayed in the family. Other scholars believe it was the prestigious religious role of the *nadītu* women, even though there is almost no information about their religious practice beside the daily and special festival offerings. Another assumption is that in some cases in the higher social class, no suitable husband was found and thus the *gagû* was an excellent alternative for the family to make sure of the daughter's future.

Nevertheless, in all the documents from and about the *nadītu* women, there is no information about their feelings toward the life in the *gagû*, or their lack of marriage and childbirth.

However, after reading thousands of letters during my academic research, I strongly believe that the essence of human nature did not really change over the past thousands of years. Therefore one could imagine that the longing for love and children must have existed just as it does today. Perhaps some of the women did lead a complete and content life in the *gagû*, but one could imagine that some may have suffered, as they would have preferred to build a family. There is one short text alluding to a *nadītu* giving birth. However we do not know what happened, if she was punished or expelled from *gagû*.

For more specific studies of the *nadītu* women and the *gagû* see:

Harris, Rivka,

"The *nadītu* Laws of the Code of Hammurapi in Praxis," *Orientalia* Vol. 30, 163-169, 1961.

"The organization and administration of the cloister in ancient Babylonia," *JESHO* 6: 121-157, 1963.

"The *Nadītu* Women," *Studies presented to A. Leo Oppenheim*, 106-135, 1964.

Ancient Sippar—A Demographic Study of an Old-Babylonian City (1894-1596 B.C.), 1975.

My use of ancient sources within fictional writing

The story was born as I was in the midst of my dissertation, in which every translation of an Akkadian source had to be verified and confirmed by references (footnotes) to other scholarly researches. Many times the ancient text was only a few lines long, while the footnotes dominated most of the page.

So when I came to insert the historical texts into the context of a fictional creation, I had to revise my way of thinking. Now my primary concern was the essence of the texts; what it added to the story or a feeling it could convey. Thus alongside trying to stay as close as possible to the original Akkadian version where possible, I had to shorten the too long and repetitive sources in a way which would agree with the rest of the book, sometimes even changing a name in order to fit the plot.

In transliterating cuneiforms it is customary to write the Akkadian in italics and the Sumerian in capital letters. Therefore I have marked those ancient texts by writing them in italic or in capital letters, in order to distinguish between them and my own new literary writing.

However, for those who would like to peek into the original sources, I offer the following references.

All letters I have cited appear in the *Altbabylonische Briefe in Umschrift und Übersetzung* (in short: **AbB**), a series of 14 volumes of letter from the Old Babylonian period in transliteration and translation. All letters in the book are of my own translations into English:

Letter in Chapter 1(AbB 1, 92); Chapter 3 (AbB 1, 129); Chapter 7 (AbB 1, 34); Chapter 14 (AbB 10, 6); Chapter 18 (AbB 14, 130).

The other sources I have brought in this book are based on translations of other scholars.

The Hymn in chapter 1 is based on the various hymns written by Enheduanna, Sargon's daughter. And see:

http://www.transoxiana.org/0108/roberts-enheduanna.html
http://www.cddc.vt.edu/feminism/Enheduanna.html
http://etcsl.orinst.ox.ac.uk/index1.htm

The story of Lahar and Ashnan in chapter 8 is based on the publication of the text in: Black, J.A., Cunningham, G., Robson, E., and G. Zólyomi, *The Electronic Text Corpus of Sumerian Literature*, Oxford.
See: http://etcsl.orinst.ox.ac.uk/section5/tr532.htm

The love poem in chapter 9 is based on two love poems translated and published by J. Thorkild, *The Harp that once. . . Sumerian Poetry in Translation*, Yale University Press, 1997.

The sales document in chapter 10 is based on a published text by K. Van Lerberghe and G. Voet in *Sippar-Amnānum, the Ur-UTU archive*, Ghent, 1991.

The creation story in chapter 13 is based on the text of *Enki and Ninmah* in J.A., Black, G., Cunningham, E., Robson, and G., Zólyomi, *The Electronic Text Corpus of Sumerian Literature*, Oxford.
See: http://etcsl.orinst.ox.ac.uk/section1/tr112.htm

All laws and extracts from the Hammurabi stele are based on the translation and publication of Martha T. Roth in *Law Collections from Mesopotamia and Asia Minor*, Atlanta, Georgia, 1995.

The letter in the epilogue is of my own making.
For further general reading and selected bibliography about the history and culture of the Ancient Near East, see *Daily Life in Ancient Mesopotamia* by Karen Rhea Nemet-Nejat, and *The Oxford Handbook of Cuneiform Culture* by Karen Radner and Eleanor Robson (ed.).

Akkadian Months

Nisānu	March/April
Āru	April/May
Simanu	May/June
Dumuzu	June/July
Abu	July/August
Ulūlu	August/September
Tišritum	September/October
Samna	October/November
Kislīmu	November/December
Ṭebētum	December/January
Šabaṭu	January/February
Addaru	February/March

About the Author

Photo credit: Eitan Herman

Shirley Graetz Ph.D. was born in Düsseldorf, Germany. In her early twenties, she went to Israel to study at the Hebrew University in Jerusalem and never left.

Later, while studying to be a tour guide, she became so fascinated with the rich history of the Ancient Near East that she decided to continue for further degrees in that field. She mastered the extinct Semitic language Akkadian while studying for her M.A. and Ph.D. in Ancient Near Eastern studies at Ben Gurion University in the Negev.

In January 2013, she received her Ph.D.

Today, Shirley is a licensed tour guide and teaches about the history of the Ancient Near East. She is married and the mother of three young children. Writing books combines two things she loves: researching history and telling stories.

You can write to her at Shirleygraetz@gmail.com.

CPSIA information can be obtained at www.ICGtesting.com
Printed in the USA
BVOW02s2315031013

332744BV00001B/31/P

9 780989 263122